W9-AAZ-152

THE FIVE ANCESTORS
OUT OF THE ASHES
Book 3

JACKAL

THE FIVE ANCESTORS
OUT OF THE ASHES
Book 3

JACKAL

JEFF STONE

Random House 🏠 New York

Text copyright © 2014 by Jeffrey S. Stone
Jacket art copyright © 2014 by Richard Cowdrey

Visit us on the Web! randomhouse.com/kids

Educators and librarians, for a variety of teaching tools, visit us at RHTeachersLibrarians.com

Library of Congress Cataloging-in-Publication Data
Stone, Jeff.
Jackal / Jeff Stone. — First edition.
   pages cm. — (The five ancestors: out of the ashes ; book 3)
Summary: When Jake is offered a chance to race in China for a world-class BMX team, he is not sure that he wants to go—but when one of his friends asks him to smuggle a mysterious drug called dragon bone that can prolong life to her dying mother in China, he feels he has to take the trip, whatever the danger.
ISBN 978-0-375-87020-0 (trade) — ISBN 978-0-375-97020-7 (lib. bdg.) —
ISBN 978-0-375-98761-8 (ebook)
1. Bicycle motocross—Juvenile fiction. 2. Friendship—Juvenile fiction. 3. Drugs—Juvenile fiction. 4. Immortalism—Juvenile fiction. 5. Adventure stories. [1. Bicycle motocross—Fiction. 2. Friendship—Fiction. 3. Drugs—Fiction. 4. Immortality—Fiction. 5. Adventure and adventurers—Fiction.] I. Title.
PZ7.S87783Jac 2014 813.6—dc23 2013033920

Printed in the United States of America
10 9 8 7 6 5 4 3 2 1
First Edition

Random House Children's Books supports the First Amendment and celebrates the right to read.

For riders who read
and readers who ride

The Five Ancestors
OUT OF THE ASHES
Book 3

JACKAL

STAGE ONE

Life is like riding a bicycle—
in order to keep your balance,
you must keep moving.

—Albert Einstein, physicist

I nosed my front tire against the starting gate and stared out at the racecourse two and a half stories below me. It was eerily similar to the men's 2012 Olympic BMX track, including an epic twenty-five-foot-high roll-in.

A man-track, with man-berms and man-jumps.

My stomach began to roil.

As a fourteen-year-old who hadn't been on a BMX bike in more than two years, I had absolutely no business riding it.

Which, of course, was exactly why I'd wanted to come. We were scheduled to leave California tonight, and I'd probably never get an opportunity like this again.

"Tear it up, Jake!" Hú Dié shouted from the bleachers.

"Show them who's boss!" Phoenix yelled from beside her.

"Get 'em, bro!" Ryan called out from beside Phoenix.

"Tighten your chinstrap, for heaven's sake!" cried Ryan's mom.

I smiled behind the rigid face mask of my rented racing helmet and adjusted my chinstrap. If I was going down in flames, at least my best friends would be there to see it, and Ryan's mom could pick up the pieces. She was good at that sort of thing.

A recorded voice boomed, *"OKAY, RIDERS, RANDOM START!"*

I glanced up the row at the seven other riders in this Sunday-morning fun race. Like me, one of them was using rented elbow and knee pads, plus a rented helmet and rented bike. Five others were wearing their own gear, including generic racing jerseys, and using bikes with mismatched parts. The last one, though—the kid in Gate 8—had a jersey plastered with sponsorship logos and a shiny new ride.

For some reason, the kid in Gate 8 nodded at me. He had smooth ebony skin and dreadlocks that crept out from the bottom of his helmet like fat snakes. I nodded back from my Gate 1 slot, just to be polite. It wasn't like I knew him. I grew up racing BMX in Southern California, and we were way north today, outside of San Francisco. I'd never ridden up here. Still, if he didn't have dreads, it could have been my old best friend Raffi. But Raffi was as bald as a beach ball when I left the state a couple years ago. People's hair didn't grow *that* fast.

"RIDERS READY . . ."

I positioned my pedals parallel to the ground and stood on them, grateful for the grippy waffle tread on the bottom of my skater shoes.

"WATCH THE GATE!"

I took a deep breath and straightened my wrists.

BEEP! BEEP! BEEP! BEEP! BEEP!

The gate dropped.

And we rolled in.

I thrust my weight forward so hard, my hips slammed into the handlebars. The bike didn't fit me perfectly, but I managed to maintain control and scorch the roll-in, my feet spinning well over a hundred revolutions per minute by the time I hit the bottom of the drop.

The seven other riders were eating my dust, including the kid from Gate 8. I grinned. The start was the most critical part of the race. I still had BMX mojo.

The first roller came faster than I expected, and I stopped pedaling, deciding what to do. It was eight feet tall, and there was a second roller after it that was positioned just the right distance to serve as a landing ramp if you wanted to jump the gap in between instead of simply rolling over them. I considered tapping the brakes because I'd promised Ryan's mom that I wouldn't catch any air, but it was too late. I hit the first roller going at least twenty miles per hour.

I shot skyward like a rocket, awakening muscle memory from years of kiddie-league BMX racing. My knees and elbows worked without me thinking about them, positioning the bike beneath me, and I leveled out.

Perfect.

I glanced down, marveling at how much sunshine was between the bottom of my tires and the ground.

From somewhere far off, Ryan's mother was screaming, "Jake, you promised! No jumping!"

Oops, I thought.

I nosed the bike down the backside of the second roller

and looked ahead. Coming up was another double roller, both at least twelve feet tall. I decided not to push my luck with Ryan's mom and tapped my brakes. I'd roll over them both instead of jumping the gap.

Out of the corner of my eye, I saw the kid from Gate 8 touch down on the backside of the second roller. Once his wheels hit the dirt, he began to pedal like a maniac.

We reached the top of the next roller at the same time. I rolled over the dirt mound, coasting lamely down the backside of it while the other kid sprang into the air like a kangaroo, pulling his bike up with him and soaring at least fifteen feet high.

Hú Dié shouted one of her banshee wails for the kid, and I frowned.

Not cool.

I began to pedal—hard. I was halfway up the second twelve-foot roller when the other kid touched down on the backside of it. He landed so smoothly that I didn't hear a sound.

He was good.

But I knew I was better.

I risked a glance over my shoulder and saw that this kid and I were smoking everyone else. I decided to ignore my promise to Ryan's mom. I kept pedaling with every ounce of strength I had while the other kid stopped pedaling in preparation for the next set of rollers—three evenly spaced twelve-footers. I watched him compress his body like a spring, and as he hit the top of the first roller, he unleashed all of that stored energy, taking flight.

I did the same thing a millisecond later, except I had

been pedaling like a beast and was traveling faster than he was when I reached the top of the roller.

He went high, but I went higher.

I was close to twenty feet off the ground, nearly the height of the massive roll-in ramp. I leveled out, passing the other kid in midair.

We both cleared the entire triple-roller gap with one jump and nosed onto the backside of the third roller with me half a bike length ahead. I'd never jumped that high or that far before. I felt like a superhero.

We transitioned directly into a tight left turn with a steeply banked berm. I leaned hard to my left and stopped pedaling so that my left pedal wouldn't dig into the dirt. I stayed low on the berm, choosing a line that was more or less a straight shot from my Gate 1 start. The other kid was way high on the berm, in line with his Gate 8 start position. However, halfway around the bend, he spun his wheel sharply in my direction and accelerated at a downward angle with incredible speed. He cut me off, stealing my line.

I tapped my brakes to avoid smashing into him and shook my head. That was a classic high/low move. I should have seen it coming. Now he was in the lead.

Next up was a series of ten equally spaced low rollers, or whoops. Most kids jumped them in pairs, but if you knew what you were doing, you could actually go faster by keeping your tires on the ground the whole time and pumping your way through them.

I knew what I was doing.

The other kid, not so much.

Or maybe he was just showing off.

The other kid took to the air, while I remained glued to the ground. I pressed down with my arms and chest, like I was doing a push-up, while also pressing down with my legs. When I began to feel myself rolling up the first whoop, I released the pressure on my legs and pulled up with my arms. Once I rolled over the top of the whoop and onto the backside, I began to press down again with all my might.

I repeated the sequence up and over the remaining rollers, and I didn't pedal the entire time. Instead, I pumped my way through the whoops with my body, picking up more speed than I thought possible. My arms and legs were beginning to ache by the end of the section, but it was worth it. The other kid may have looked cooler, pogoing through the whoops and jumping them in pairs, but I zipped over the last one a full bike length ahead of him. Now I was in the lead.

Next up was another turn, this one to the right. The bend wasn't as sharp as the last one, and the berm wasn't anywhere near as steep. However, this turn had something I'd never seen before in a BMX track—a jump at the very center of it.

I whizzed around the first half of the bend and hit the lip of the turn-jump going faster than I should have. I not only cleared the gap, I nearly jumped *out* of the entire track. Fortunately, there was a safety wall made of solid plywood at the top of the berm, and I hit it square on with both tires. I rode the wall for a few feet like a street BMXer cruising along the side of a building. Then I bunny-hopped off and righted my bike, putting the wheels back on the dirt.

THE FIVE ANCESTORS OUT OF THE ASHES

I blinked several times to make sure I wasn't dreaming. That was probably the sickest move I'd ever pulled off.

The other kid had timed the jump much better, and he caught up with me. We rode neck and neck, flying over more sets of eight- and twelve-foot rollers before zipping into the final turn—another tight one to the left.

I took the turn high this time, while the other kid stayed low. The low road was the shortest route, which usually made it the best choice. However, as the other kid's earlier move had reminded me, a high rider could gather more speed on a turn like this by taking advantage of the berm's steep downward angle. I decided to give it a go.

I swept down the berm like a hawk, but the other kid saw me coming. He began to pedal furiously while leaning hard to his left.

Pedaling on a berm was dangerous. The kid handled it like a pro, though, his left foot and pedal barely skimming the dirt's surface. He inched forward, preventing me from getting in front of him.

I settled for riding at his side as we completed the turn and headed for the final straightaway, which consisted of another section of ten whoops, followed by a pair of twelve-foot rollers. After that was the finish line.

I pumped the whoops like I'd done on the previous set, but so did the other kid. His upper body was clearly stronger than mine because he began to creep ahead. By the time we finished the whoops and reached the top of the first twelve-foot roller, he was out in front by half a bike length.

I was going to lose.

We went airborne, and I ground my teeth. I didn't mind

losing a race on a mountain bike or road bike, but for some reason I couldn't stomach losing on a BMX bike. This was *my* territory. Somewhere very far off, Hú Dié let loose another one of her banshee wails, and I knew that it was meant to motivate me. I had to do something.

I squeezed my bike frame between my knees and tail-whipped my rear tire in the direction of the other rider. Skilled racers do this all the time as a neat trick. However, unskilled racers do it, too, most often because they've lost control of their bike.

The other kid saw my rear tire headed his way, and he flinched. His smooth glide became an erratic wobble. I pulled my rear tire back underneath me, beginning to regret what I'd just done.

I landed as soft as a feather, while the other rider slammed into the backside of the final roller like a rookie. Thankfully, he didn't go down, but he'd lost most of his speed.

As I coasted to victory, I looked over my shoulder, because I wanted to make sure that the other kid was okay. Unfortunately, he appeared to take it as me being cocky and waved an angry fist at me.

I stopped well beyond the finish line to give the other kid and the remaining riders plenty of room to complete the race, but the kid with the dreadlocks kept coming toward me—fast. Hard. And I had nowhere to go. My back was against a plywood wall.

I couldn't help thinking of Ryan's crash into a fellow racer, and the final outcome. I braced myself, preparing for the worst.

2

I heard brakes squeal and tires swoosh as the rider on the shiny new bike cut his front wheel an instant before plowing into me. His rear tire skidded around, scraping off the top layer of the track and sending up a wave of dirt that clogged my nostrils and clouded my vision. I choked out loud.

The kid laughed. "Better watch yourself, Jake. Paybacks are rough."

I tore off my helmet and shook my head, using my shaggy blond hair to mop some of the dirt from my face. The other rider removed his helmet, too.

I rubbed my eyes. "Raffi? It *is* you!"

"The one and only," he said.

"How'd your hair get so long?"

"Extensions, yo. Now introduce me to your crew before things get ugly."

I looked over Raffi's shoulder and saw my friends running toward us at full speed, forcing the remaining six riders off the track as soon as they crossed the finish line. Phoenix's eyes glowed with green fire, and Hú Dié and Ryan appeared ready to smash something.

I held up both hands and yelled, "Easy, guys! This is Raffi. He's just messing with me. He was my best friend before I moved to Indiana."

"I'm messing with *you*?" Raffi said, adjusting his sweet dreadlocks. "What about that tail whip?"

"Sorry, bro," I replied, "but you started it by high/lowing me on the first turn."

Raffi chuckled. "Oh, yeah. My bad."

Phoenix, Ryan, and Hú Dié stopped next to me. They were all panting from their effort, and they didn't look happy. It was, like, ninety degrees out, and they were sweating buckets.

"Everything's cool?" Phoenix asked.

"Cool as a cucumber," I said.

"You gonna introduce us?" Raffi asked.

"You know it," I said, pointing. "That's Phoenix, that's Ryan, and that's Hú Dié."

Raffi smiled, his teeth gleaming. "Nice to meet you all, though I already know who you are."

Phoenix raised a sweaty eyebrow. "Really?"

"Sure. You guys are all over the Internet, man. I normally don't pay attention to road bike racing, but I saw Jake's pic on the local newspaper's home page, and I had to investigate." He turned to me. "You got mad BMX skills, yo. Why you fooling with road bikes?"

"Because he is *good* at it," Hú Dié answered. "The road bike race he won the other night was against adults."

"I read that," Raffi said, "and I also read that you came in second. Pretty impressive."

I saw a hint of a smile appear on Hú Dié's face. "Thank you," she said.

She was wearing shorts in the July heat, and I pointed to her burly quads. "Hú Dié drops hammers."

"No doubt," Raffi said. "You ride any other kinds of bikes besides road bikes, Hú Dié? Maybe BMX?"

"I ride here and there," she replied.

"Don't be so modest," Ryan said. "She's a monster on any kind of bike. She even builds them by hand in a bike shop she owns in China."

"That is so cool," Raffi said.

"I am really not that great on a BMX bike, though," Hú Dié said, "especially when it comes to tricks." She rested her hand on my shoulder. "But Jake . . . I had no idea you could ride like that! *I* am the one who is impressed!"

I felt my cheeks begin to turn red. "It's nothing, really. Raffi and I used to do a little riding."

"A little riding?" Raffi said. "That's the understatement of the century, yo! We used to ride at least five days a week, two or three hours a day. Sometimes more."

"During summer vacation?" Phoenix asked.

"Nah, man, during the school year. Check it—Jake's folks are both busy lawyers, right? Mine are both doctors. Every day after school, a van used to pick us and a couple other kids up and take us to the local BMX track. We'd do our homework, eat a snack, and then ride until our folks got us. We all got real good at racing and doing BMX tricks and stuff, but your boy Jake here was always the best."

"Now you're the one who's exaggerating," I said.

"It's true," Raffi said, raising his right hand. "I swear."

I glanced at his long-sleeved racing jersey. "I don't think I've ever seen so many sponsor logos on a BMX jersey before. You pro now?"

"Not yet. Sponsors are flowing all kinds of gear to kids nowadays, even if they're not pro. I bet you'd be pro by now if you'd stuck with racing."

"Hey, you kids!" someone announced with a bullhorn. *"Clear the track! We have another heat to run."*

"Sorry!" we yelled back, hurrying away from the finish line with Raffi in tow. We headed for the concession stand, where Ryan's mother was waiting for us. She was hard to miss. Her body got messed up from taking some kind of bad experimental weight-loss drug, and no matter how little she ate, she kept gaining weight. I felt bad for her.

Ryan's mom frowned. "I was wondering when you kids would show up. Jake could probably use a little hydration after all that jumping. I hear the air is drier in the upper atmosphere."

"I'm really sorry, Mrs. Vanderhausen," I said. "I got carried away out there."

"It is what it is, Jake. Turn in your bike and your gear. You're done. We're leaving now."

"But, Mom!" Ryan said. "We all planned to rent bikes and do a race or two for fun."

"Absolutely not," Ryan's mom said. "Jake's parents signed the waiver, but I have yet to hear back from Phoenix's grandfather. I won't put my name on the line for him in a place like this, and I certainly won't put my name on the line for you. You could *die* on that track! I've been involved in cycling most of my adult life, and I've never seen anything like it."

"Most tracks aren't this crazy, Mrs. Vanderhausen," I said.

"Which, I suppose, is why you wanted to ride it?"

I shrugged.

"Come on, Mom," Ryan said.

"No," she replied. "You probably shouldn't be riding yet, anyway. Hok said that you should take it easy."

"I'm fine," Ryan said. "I told you last night, I haven't felt this good in months."

"My answer is still no."

Ryan shook his head. "What about Hú Dié? She's eighteen."

Ryan's mom laughed. "That's what her passport says, but I know better. Now all of you, say goodbye to your new friend . . . what's your name, son?"

"Raffi," he said, sticking out his hand. "Jake is an old friend of mine. We used to ride BMX together down in Southern California."

Ryan's mom shook Raffi's hand. "Pleased to meet you, Raffi. Where are your parents?"

"Working. My dad's delivering a baby and my mom's doing an emergency appendectomy. This place is my home away from home. I have a question, ma'am. If these guys can't ride the track, would you consider letting them ride a small loop?"

"What do you mean?"

Raffi gestured toward a patch of woods a few hundred yards away, across an open farm field. "There's a short trail over there. You don't need a waiver or anything."

"How short?" Ryan's mom asked.

"It's a seventy-five-yard loop. The track we just rode is more than five hundred yards long."

"Are there jumps?"

"Not exactly," Raffi said. "It's a pump track. You don't even pedal when you ride it."

"How big are the—what do you call them—*whoops*?"

"Different sizes, but the biggest one is smaller than the smallest roller me and Jake just raced over."

Ryan's mom wiped her sweaty brow and checked her watch. "I don't know, this place is farther outside of the city than I originally thought."

"Please, Mom?" Ryan said. "It will be a chance for me to stretch my legs. I'll prove to you that I'm fine. I haven't been on any kind of bike since the road bike race."

Ryan's mom sighed. "I suppose I could give you kids an hour, if you want. We should still have time to shower back at the hotel and get to the airport. We've already said our goodbyes."

"All right!" Ryan said. "What do you guys think?"

"I'll do it," I said.

"I would love to," Hú Dié said. "I have never been on a pump track."

Phoenix didn't answer. He was staring across the parking lot at something.

I poked him. "Phoenix?"

"Huh?" Phoenix said. "Oh, I've never been on a pump track, either, but I'm game."

"Then it's settled," Ryan said. "Let's rent some bikes and gear and get rolling!"

Ryan's mom decided to wait in her rental van while the rest of us jumped on our rented BMX bikes and followed Raffi across the field, toward the patch of woods.

The bumpy ground reminded me why BMX bikes weren't as popular as mountain bikes. A mountain bike's larger diameter tires rolled over bumps much easier and acted kind of like shock absorbers. More than that, many mountain bikes had actual shock absorbers built into the front forks and sometimes even the rear-wheel supports. It really smoothed out the ride. But what a mountain bike gained in smoothness, it lacked in sprinting speed and handling. A completely rigid BMX bike allowed all of your power to be transferred to the rear tire, and the smaller bike size and tire diameter meant that you could maneuver it a million times better. I'd take speed and handling over a cushy ride any day.

We reached the woods, and I saw that it was larger than

I'd imagined. It was a couple hundred yards square and surrounded on all sides by farm fields. Raffi said that the woods and farm fields were owned by the same people who owned the BMX track. They wanted to create a place for kids to hang out away from the city, so they sectioned off part of their farm and used their farming equipment to push dirt around until they came up with the Olympic-like track he and I had just ridden. It became so popular, the people then built the roll-in ramp with a starting gate, concession stand, bleachers, and bike rental shack. Running it took more than a hundred volunteers.

I wasn't sure if the landowners knew about the pump track in the woods, and I wasn't about to ask Raffi if they knew, either. Back in the day, Raffi and I had trespassed more than once to build dirt jumps in parks or on abandoned property.

We followed Raffi along a well-worn trail fifty yards or so into the trees. Then we stopped beside the most beautifully sculpted mounds of dirt I'd ever laid eyes on.

Hú Dié gasped. "This is amazing!"

"You *built* this?" I asked.

"Yep," Raffi said proudly. "I had some help from my crew, though."

I was blown away. The pump track looked better than some of the ones I'd seen on DVDs and online videos, including those built by professional BMX trail builders. The lines were amazing, and the flow was so strong it just about sucked you in. Some of the rollers were chill, while others were so steep that they could only be called ramps. Each takeoff ramp had a perfectly positioned landing ramp, and it was clear that a person could pump endless loops around this thing without ever pedaling.

"I can't believe it," Ryan said. "What did you use to build it?"

Raffi reached down and lifted an old canvas tarp. "These. Nothing but hand shovels, rakes, and watering cans."

"Incredible," Phoenix said. "How many people did it take?"

"About a dozen kids. I'm the oldest, just turned fifteen. I'm basically the ringleader. This track is my design."

"You da man, Raffi!" I said. "How long have you been working on it?"

"Almost two years. That's when my folks and I moved up here."

"Sweet," I said. "Who else knows about this place?"

"No one, and we want to keep it that way. You're the first outsiders to come here. We especially don't want adults to see it. Fortunately, the landowners are old and don't get around much. They know we have a trail out here, but I doubt they've ever bothered to come look at it."

"I'll bet you a million dollars they've never seen it," I said. "This is totally rad! Later!"

I rolled my bike onto the track.

"Hold up," Raffi said. "We've got to water it down first."

I looked back at him. "Why?"

"It's way dry today, man. You remember the drill down in So Cal, right? Hours of packing dirt for a few minutes of riding."

"But we do not have hours," Hú Dié said.

"No worries," Raffi said. "There's a stream close by. If we each grab a watering can, we'll be done in no time."

I sighed and rolled my bike back off of the track. "Fine, let's get to work."

Twenty minutes later, we'd finished watering and packing the pump track. We were ready to rock.

I hit the track first, with Raffi close behind. We were going to ride in a line, each rider doing a different trick than the next. It was fun to do and looked really cool.

Hú Dié and Ryan decided to sit on the sidelines and watch a few laps before joining in, while Phoenix said that he had to pee. He tromped off into the woods to take care of his business.

The pump track was all that I'd hoped it would be, and more. The low rollers and berms turned out to be perfect practice for BMX racing, while the steep seven-foot-tall ramps provided more than enough height to pull off wicked tricks like 360-degree tail whips, bar spins, and tabletops. Halfway around my first lap, I was ready to sell my clunky, oversized mountain bike and buy a sweet little BMX bike. At the end of one full lap, I swore I would build a track just like this the minute we got home.

After Raffi and I did a few laps, Hú Dié was ready to join us. Ryan wasn't sure he could handle all of the jumps, so he said that he would just watch for now. Hú Dié rolled onto the track, and—

"*OOOWWWWW!*"

Someone screamed in pain.

The scream stopped abruptly, and a deep voice boomed in a foreign language that sounded like Chinese.

"Tíngzhǐ!"

Raffi and I skidded to a stop, while Hú Dié ditched her bike without even bothering to slow down. She shouted, "Phoenix!"

"Was that Chinese?" I asked.

"Yes!" Hú Dié replied as she ran over to the pile of tools.

"What did he say?"

"Stop!" she replied, grabbing a flathead shovel and taking off in the direction of the cry.

Raffi looked at me. "Is that girl crazy?"

"You have no idea, bro," I said, and dropped my bike. "Come on!"

I ran over to the tools, grabbed a shovel, and headed after Hú Dié. Ryan had already grabbed a rake and was running after her. Raffi dropped his bike and grabbed a rake, too.

"I'll stay here and guard our stuff!" Raffi yelled.

"Good idea!" I shouted back.

Hú Dié, Ryan, and I ran at least a hundred yards before I realized that we'd reached the opposite end of the woods. There was a black Jeep parked where the woods met a plowed field. Two Asian men were getting out of the Jeep. One guy was short and fat; the other was a gigantic bodybuilder type. Both wore suits and ties despite the heat. They left their doors open, and I could hear their air conditioner fan blasting from within the vehicle.

CRACK!

I swiveled my head toward the sound and saw that Hú Dié was holding just her shovel's wooden handle. She'd wedged the flat blade into the fork of a thick tree trunk and snapped the long handle clean off. She leaped out of the woods, into the field, and began to spin the shovel handle in front of her like a kung fu staff.

"Phoenix!" Hú Dié shouted. "Where are you?"

"Over here!" he replied from somewhere behind us. "I'm fine! I'm still in the woods! Watch out for the guys in the Jeep! I just took out a dude who was creeping around, spying on us."

The bodybuilder guy slid his hand beneath his suit jacket and pulled out a pistol. He took a step toward Phoenix's voice, and Hú Dié attacked.

She covered the distance between her and the huge guy in three long strides. He took a giant step backward to create some space but bumped into the open Jeep door behind him. It caused him to stumble for an instant, and that was all the time Hú Dié needed.

Quick as lightning, she brought the spinning piece of wood down on the guy's meaty gun hand. He swore and dropped the weapon, and Hú Dié swung the shovel handle like a baseball bat at the guy's head.

The guy raised one massive forearm to block the blow, and the shovel handle snapped in half, leaving Hú Dié with only three feet of splintered wood. The guy reached for her throat, and she stabbed at his huge hand with the splintered end. He pulled his hand back, pivoting away from her; then I heard Ryan shout.

I looked over to see him sprinting toward the big guy. Ryan raised his rake and brought it down hard, slashing at the man's head.

The big guy caught the rake's shaft with both hands. He yanked at the rake, but Ryan held fast. Ryan was crazy strong, too. As the two of them wrestled for control of the rake, Hú Dié raised both of her forearms and smashed them into the sides of the big guy's head as if she were crushing a walnut with a nutcracker.

The big guy went down. He wasn't getting back up anytime soon, either. Hú Dié's full name means *Iron Butterfly* in Chinese, and she practiced some sort of Iron Kung Fu training on her forearms.

The short, fat guy on the other side of the Jeep said something in Chinese. His voice was deep and calm, and his tone sounded like he was used to being the boss.

Hú Dié seemed to relax a little bit.

Ryan and I turned to her.

"What did he say?" Ryan asked.

"He, uh, complimented me," she replied. "He said maybe he should consider hiring me as his bodyguard instead of the guy I just knocked out."

The fat guy nodded and gestured toward the woods.

"Oh, no!" I said. "Phoenix!"

The three of us hurried into the trees while the fat guy followed, taking his time.

We found Phoenix on the ground with his legs wrapped tightly around the torso of a skinny, young Asian man. The man was lying on his side, and Phoenix was latched to his back. He wore a fancy suit like the other two guys, and his gold wire-rimmed glasses were askew. He was trying to talk, but he wasn't having much success because Phoenix had one arm wrapped around his throat from behind in a chokehold.

Raffi was standing next to Phoenix, looking totally confused. He stared at me in disbelief. "This Phoenix kid is as crazy as Hú Dié!"

I nodded. "Pretty much. I thought you were going to stay with the bikes."

"I heard more shouts and decided to come help," Raffi said, holding his rake. "It looks like you all have things under control, though. What the heck is going on?"

"I have no idea," I said. "Phoenix?"

"Don't ask me," Phoenix replied. "I busted this guy creeping up on us. I didn't really have to pee, you know. I saw three Asian dudes in that Jeep back by the track. They looked suspicious and seemed to be watching us. I thought I heard a vehicle driving through the field while we were working on the pump track, so I snuck back here and found this clown. He looked like he was going for a knife, so I took him down. It turned out to be a fancy pen, but whatever. I was going to let him go, but then I heard you guys fighting someone. I figured I'd hang on to him, just in case."

"Hú Dié knocked one of the dudes out," I said. "He was a bodyguard. The other one is right behind us."

The fat guy ambled over and grinned. He pointed at Phoenix, then said something in Chinese to Hú Dié.

Hú Dié sighed and turned to Phoenix. "Nice going. You just choked out the only one who speaks English."

"He's not completely out," Phoenix said. "He's just . . ."

Phoenix glanced at the skinny man and frowned. He had indeed slipped into unconsciousness. Phoenix let go of the man's neck, and his head lolled to one side. At least he was still breathing. His narrow chest expanded and contracted beneath his suit jacket. Phoenix unlatched his legs from around the man's midsection and stood.

The fat guy said something else in Chinese.

Hú Dié looked at him suspiciously; then she looked at us. "This guy says that while he is impressed with our kung fu skills, he and the other two men mean us no harm."

"Then why were they sneaking up on us?" Phoenix asked.

Hú Dié repeated the question in Chinese, and the fat guy gave her a long answer. Hú Dié's face took on a look of concern. When he finished talking, he smiled broadly— at me.

"What?" I said.

"He says that he is the boss," Hú Dié explained. "He apologizes for approaching us in this manner. He actually came to talk with you, Jake."

"Me? Why?"

"He wants you to race for him. In China."

I chuckled. "That's whacked. Tell him no thanks."

Hú Dié shook her head. "You do not understand. He told me who he is, and who he works for. I think it would be in your best interest to hear what the other guy has to say in English once he wakes up."

"Why?"

Hú Dié swallowed hard. "Because it is supposedly an offer you cannot refuse."

I stared at Hú Dié, trying my best to figure out what she was saying. *An offer I cannot refuse?*

Dragon bone immediately came to mind, and my heart sank. I'd thought that junk was out of my life for good. But what else could it be? These guys were Chinese, after all.

Dragon bone was a freaky Chinese herbal medicine made from ground-up fossils that people claimed came from actual dragons. It supposedly gave you superhuman powers. As if.

The crazy thing was, though, Ryan had taken some in order to make him ride faster, and it really did make him go faster—until it nearly killed him. It nearly killed a bunch of other people, too, including Phoenix's grandfather. The poor guy has to take it every day, because if he ever stops, he'll die. The last thing I wanted was to get mixed up with the stuff.

The skinny Asian man that Phoenix had choked groaned

and slowly sat up, brushing dirt off of his face. I noticed a large bruise forming there, as if he'd been punched.

"Ooooohhh, dear me," he said in perfect English. "I am so light-headed."

"Take shallow breaths," Phoenix said. "If you breathe too deeply, you might pass out again."

The man nodded, and I glanced over at Hú Dié, Ryan, and Raffi. They'd formed a wide circle around the short, fat Chinese guy. He'd said that he meant us no harm, but my friends obviously weren't taking any chances. That was another thing I hated about dragon bone. Violence followed wherever it went.

Phoenix pulled a fancy pen from one of the pockets in his cargo shorts and handed it to the skinny man. "You'd better be careful with this. I thought it was a knife."

The man rubbed his jaw. "Is that why you socked me?"

"No," Phoenix replied. "I socked you because you were stalking me and my friends. I choked you because of the pen."

"I apologize if you thought I was a stalker. I can assure you, this is not the case. I simply wanted to speak with you and your friends, and with Jake in particular."

"Then why didn't you come talk with us back at the main track?" Ryan asked.

The skinny man stood on shaky legs. "To be honest, we were taken aback by what we saw. We followed your van to the track from downtown San Francisco—which I'll admit is rather like stalking—but we only wanted to talk with you about road bike racing. Once we saw what Jake could do on a BMX bike, well, that changed our plans. By the time we were ready to approach you, you'd already headed for this patch of woods. We intended to follow you by driving along the same path you took through the field, but then we saw a proper road leading here. It meant a bit of a hike through the woods on foot for me, but by taking the road, our vehicle wouldn't disrupt the fields. We were being considerate of the landowners."

"You should learn to be more considerate of *us*," Phoenix said.

"I see that now. Your kung fu is very good."

"What do you *really* want?" I asked. "If this has anything to do with dragon bone—"

"Dragon bone?" the skinny man asked. "Dear me, no. We've come to discuss bicycle racing. Specifically, you racing for a Chinese national team. You *and* your friends, Jake."

"Huh?" I said. "Hú Dié is the only one who is Chinese."

"Exactly. Allow me to introduce myself. My name is Ling, and this"—he gestured toward the short, fat guy—"is Mr. Chang. He is the head of a special committee that has been set up to try to popularize bicycle racing in China. China is a powerhouse in many professional and Olympic sports, but bicycle racing is in its infancy in our county. Hundreds of millions of Chinese people ride bicycles every day, but few actually compete on them and fewer still do it outside of Asia. It's rather silly, to be honest, but the simple truth is that most Chinese people don't know about the opportunities available to race bicycles, whether it's road bikes, mountain bikes, cyclocross bikes, BMX bikes, or velodrome bikes. It's Mr. Chang's job to fix that."

"What does this have to do with me?"

"We need a poster boy, Jake. We're going to focus on recruiting kids, and who better to celebrate than a boy who just beat a field of adults? Never mind that you are not a Chinese citizen. The fact that you're American will actually *help* our cause. You are the perfect candidate. Not only can you ride, but you also have the perfect look. Your appearance is consistent with that of a California surfer. Everyone loves a surfer, especially Chinese girls." He winked. "You'll have more girlfriends than you'll know what to do with."

I felt myself begin to blush.

"He is right, Jake," Hú Dié said. "About the girls, and about bike racing. I have been wishing my entire life that bike racing was more popular in China. I would love to be able to race every summer weekend like you guys do here in the States."

Mr. Chang pointed to Hú Dié and said something in Chinese. This time, she was the one who blushed. The fat man grinned.

"What did he say?" Raffi asked.

"Mr. Chang complimented my looks as well as my riding," Hú Dié said. "He also complimented Ryan and Phoenix. He is certain we would all be famous across China."

"What do you have in mind?" I asked.

"We want the four of you to race together," Ling said. "We'd like a poster team as much as a poster boy, if we can have it. In addition to your all-American surfer looks, Jake, Ryan has the powerful European physique, Phoenix has his unique green-eyed, red-haired Chinese/Caucasian appearance, and Hú Dié is clearly strong yet possesses a classic Chinese beauty. You are not only a talented bunch, you're a marketing dream. I wouldn't be surprised if your fame were to spread beyond China, across the entire world."

I saw a glimmer in the eyes of all three of my friends. Even Raffi seemed stoked.

"Yo, Jake," Raffi said. "If this dude is for real, you should seriously consider his offer."

I shook my head. "I don't know. It sounds too much like work to me."

Raffi snapped his fingers. "That's right. I forgot. You hate to work. Otherwise, you'd be the one wearing the BMX jersey with all the sponsor logos instead of me." He rolled his eyes. "Don't hate me for this, Jake, but you've got to stop being so lazy. You could really do something with this."

"You don't get it," I said. "I worked really hard the past few weeks, learning to race road bikes. It was fun, and I won a race. Big deal. I'm already over it. You probably don't know this, but first place in that race came with a professional sponsorship. I told them that I wasn't interested, and they were glad because they didn't want a kid. I'd rather ride a BMX bike or even a mountain bike instead of a road bike, any day. Road bikes are kind of . . . boring."

Ling grinned. "That's exactly what we were discussing in the parking lot. We drove out here expecting to invite you to China as a four-person road racing team. However, seeing you ride BMX broadened our focus. I recalled reading stories of the four of you racing mountain bikes in Indiana as well as Ryan and Phoenix training for cyclocross in Texas. We've decided that we'd like the four of you to participate as a team in a road race in Shanghai this Saturday. Afterward, we'll arrange for all of you to participate in different types of cycling races throughout the rest of the year, depending upon your interest level and skills. The four of you already have a fair amount of media exposure in China because of your victory the other night in San Francisco, combined with your brush with gangsters in Chinatown, which was all over the Chinese newspapers. We can use that. You will be stars. You'll be asked to sign more autographs after the race than the rest of the participants combined. I guarantee it."

"I don't care about being famous," I said, "especially if it has anything to do with those Chinese gangsters. I don't even care about winning races. I just want to have fun with my friends."

"It sounds like it *would* be fun, Jake," Phoenix said.

"Yeah," Ryan said. "It would be a riot."

I sighed and looked at Hú Dié. "What do you think?"

She smiled. "It would be my dream come true, but this is not about me. What do *you* want?"

"I just want to ride my bike, bros," I said. "I don't care about racing. I want to go home and chill with you guys for the next two weeks. That's all the summer vacation we have left."

"Think of it this way," Ling said. "If you accept our offer, your summer vacation will *never* end. You'll be enrolled in an American-style school, but you won't be there much. You'll be too busy racing and making public appearances. Your schedule will be like that of college athletes."

"Hang on," I said. "How long do you expect me to stay in China?"

"At least one year. More than likely, two or three."

"That's insane! No way."

"It's not that insane," Ryan said. "I spent six months training in Belgium. The time flew by, and even though my uncle was a jerk, I still had a lot of fun. Living in a foreign country is cool."

"It *is* cool," Phoenix said, "especially China. I was only there for a few days, but I could tell that it would be neat to live in a big city like Shanghai if I had some friends to hang out with."

"And I would be there to translate for everyone," Hú Dié said. "Oh, Jake! We would have the best time ever!"

I shook my head. "I'm still not feeling it."

Ling removed a business card from the pocket of his suit jacket and held it out to me. "Why don't you take a day and think about it? We can't wait any longer than that. The Shanghai race is coming up fast."

"What if I say no?" I asked. "Would my friends still be able to join your team?"

"No. We need a winner, Jake. You won the race. Our plan won't work without you."

"Hey," Phoenix said. "I have an idea. How about Jake only commits to a week in China? It would be like a trial run. We all go and do the race, and Jake gets a chance to see how he likes it."

"Hmmm," Ling said. "Just a moment." He turned to Mr. Chang, and they spoke in Chinese for a minute. Ling turned back to us and said, "We could do one week."

I took the business card from Ling. "I'll think it over. Don't get your hopes up, though."

Ling nodded. "Remember, I'll need your answer by tomorrow night, at the very latest."

"Okay."

Raffi pulled a cell phone from his pocket and tapped the screen. "Yo," he said. "I hate to be a party pooper, but don't you all have a plane to catch?"

Ryan glanced at his training watch. "We don't actually fly out until really late, but it does look like our hour is up. Bummer. I guess I'll have to find a BMX trail somewhere in Indiana to see if I can fly like you guys."

"You're welcome to come back here anytime," Raffi said. "All of you."

"Thanks, bro," I said. "I'd like to do that, especially if I take a pass on China. Any chance we could all come and crash at your place over fall break or something?"

"Are you kidding me?" Raffi said. "My mom still asks after you, even though she knows we lost touch. Your friends seem solid, too. You're in."

"Awesome," I said. "Did you change your phone number when you moved?"

"Nope," Raffi said. "I still have the same digits. So do my folks."

"Sweet. I'll be in touch." I turned to Phoenix, Ryan, and Hú Dié. "Come on, guys. Let's go home."

5

The rest of the day flew by, and we boarded the plane to Indiana without any drama. I buckled in for the four-and-a-half-hour overnight flight, sitting next to Ryan and his mom. Less than fifteen minutes after takeoff, they were both sound asleep.

I wasn't surprised. It was midnight, and half the people on the plane had already nodded off. I'd forgotten to charge my computer tablet after using it at the airport, so I flipped on the overhead light and poked through the seat pocket in front of me for something to eyeball. I found a copy of a San Francisco newspaper from the previous day. One of the headlines read:

SEARCH FOR CYCLIST'S BODY CALLED OFF

I frowned and unfolded the paper to take a closer look.

SAN FRANCISCO—Authorities have called off the search for the remains of controversial professional cyclist Lin Tan. His body disappeared during an investigation into the death of a Chinatown resident and reputed Chinese mafia kingpin known only as DuSow.

DuSow, literally *Poison Hand* in Chinese, was found strangled to death outside his wharf-front warehouse immediately following last week's nighttime criterium bicycle race. According to security surveillance video and eyewitness accounts, he was killed by one of his former associates, DaXing, who is still at large.

Lin Tan's body was found at the scene, and the same eyewitnesses claim he fell victim to DuSow's reputed ability to poison someone simply by touching his victim's skin. Preliminary tests of DuSow's remains suggest these reports may be plausible, and skin discoloration on areas of Lin Tan's remains are consistent with that of death by poison.

Lin Tan's body was photographed at the scene by an EMT who failed to locate a pulse. Because of concerns over secondhand poison transfer, the body was temporarily left where it lay—draped over the railing of DuSow's sailboat, *The Strong Hold*. Authorities believe that at some unknown point during the investigation, Lin Tan's body slipped off of the railing, into San Francisco Bay, where powerful currents washed it out to sea.

The Coast Guard has been patrolling the bay since the incident, but to no avail. As of this morning, all search efforts have been suspended. Lin Tan's death has been officially ruled a homicide, and the investigation is still open.

I folded the newspaper and shoved it back into the seat pocket. What horrible news. It seemed every time I turned around, dragon bone reared its ugly head. The stuff wasn't mentioned in the article, but that was only because Ryan, his mom, Phoenix, and I, along with several others, had done such a good job of conveniently forgetting to bring it up to investigators. The truth was, both DuSow and Lin Tan were dead because of dragon bone, and so were lots of other people. I'd argued with Phoenix that telling the police was the best way to get dragon bone out of our lives for good, but in the end I caved to his pleas that we all keep our mouths shut.

Phoenix was a great guy, but he could be clueless sometimes. He did whatever his grandfather told him to do. His grandfather wanted to keep dragon bone secret, because he knew that his life would be changed forever if word got out that he was four hundred years old, thanks to dragon bone. I would never have believed the old man's true age if I hadn't seen what I'd seen over the past few weeks. Dragon bone was truly some messed-up stuff.

I turned off my overhead light and shut my eyes, trying to think happier thoughts. As cheesy as it sounds, the first thing that came to mind was my parents. I liked them. A lot. I mean, sure, my mom talked too much and my dad was kind of hyper, but they took good care of me and were really great to hang out with. I just wished we got to hang out more often. Like Raffi said, they were super busy people.

Even so, I felt lucky. None of my friends had "normal" homes. Ryan's dad had passed away from cancer less than a year ago, and he lived with just his mom. Hú Dié's mom was in an assisted-living facility because she had ALS—Lou Gehrig's disease—so it was just Hú Dié and her dad at home. Both of Phoenix's parents had died in a car wreck when he was a baby, and he lived with his grandfather. If there was one thing I couldn't complain about, it was two solid parents.

My folks knew most of what had happened in San Francisco, but I never told them about dragon bone. It wasn't so much because of the bad guys involved, but the good guys—like Ryan, a wise old Chinese woman named Hok who lived in San Francisco's Chinatown, and even Phoenix's grandfather. I knew how careful my parents were about legal issues, and I'm positive they'd never let me hang out with *any* of my friends again if they knew what I knew. More than that, if my parents ever found out that I'd withheld important information from investigators, they'd kill me.

I'd talked with my mom for, like, an hour before our flight took off, and it was nice to hear her voice. As usual, she did most of the talking, motor-mouthing about the weather and other nonsense, but that's exactly what I needed back in my life—a major dose of normal. I did tell her about Ling and Mr. Chang's offer for me to be China's "poster boy" for cycling, and she actually went quiet for a full ten seconds. Then she rambled on about how she thought it would be a great idea for me to take them up on the offer to try for a week. She said that she and my father were going to be swamped for the next month anyway, and that I might as well be off doing something exciting with my friends instead of sitting around the house, bored. I told her the same thing I'd told Ling, that I'd think about it.

My mom said that while she couldn't pick me up from the Indianapolis airport when we landed—at 7:30 a.m., because of the time change—she'd be home when Ryan's mom dropped me off around 8:30 a.m. My dad was going to be home, too. Best of all, my mom was going to make her famous huevos rancheros for breakfast. I couldn't remember the last time the three of us had eaten a meal together. I was pumped.

I thought I heard people arguing softly in the row across from me, and I opened my eyes just a hair. It turned out to be Phoenix and Hú Dié, who were sitting beside one another. I doubted I'd ever figure those two out. Sometimes they acted like best friends. Other times they fought like brother and sister, complete with fists flying. I didn't have any brothers or sisters, which was why my friends meant so much to me. Phoenix had been my best friend until this summer vacation began. Now he, Ryan, and Hú Dié were pretty equal in the best-friend department, and I liked it that way. I hoped that whatever I decided about China didn't screw that up.

It was obvious that the three of them were ready to move to China immediately and start racing for Mr. Chang. I wasn't sure what I wanted to do yet. At least, that's what I told them and myself. Deep down, though, I knew the truth. There was no way I was going to a foreign country to race bikes, even for a week. I wasn't even sure that I wanted to race bikes in the good old USA anymore. Riding Raffi's dirt trail reminded me that bikes were supposed to be fun. Racing was too much work.

Ryan and his mom both began to snore, and I couldn't help grinning. At least they had their priorities right. I couldn't do anything about any of the stuff on my mind while I was thirty thousand feet in the air, so I might as well get some sleep. I closed my eyes again and tried to follow Ryan's mom's lead. If everything went well, I'd be home before I knew it.

"Hi!" I shouted. "I'm home!"

"We're in the kitchen, baby!"

I smiled, closing the back door behind me. I dropped my key into the pocket of my cargo shorts, dragged my suitcase into the mudroom, and headed for the main hallway. The house smelled *awesome*.

"Perfect timing!" my dad said as I left the hallway and entered the kitchen. "So glad you're home." He hugged me, squashing my face against his fancy silk tie. He must have been going to court. He was an environmental attorney, and usually just wore jeans and a t-shirt to the office.

My mom stepped away from the stove and wrapped me in a massive bear hug, even though she was no bigger than an average high school girl. She wore a fancy apron over even fancier business clothes. The apron smelled like fresh chilies and fried corn tortillas. My mouth began to water.

"It is *so* nice to have you home," my mom said as she

released me and went back to cooking. "How was your flight?"

"Great," I said. "I slept through most of it."

"Attaboy," my dad said. "It will help with the jet lag. Any new developments since we last spoke?"

I thought about the article I'd read on the plane concerning Lin Tan, but I wasn't in the mood to talk about it. "Nope," I said.

"That's good," my mom said. "Have you given China any more thought?"

"Yeah, I've decided that I don't want to go."

My parents glanced at one another, and my dad plopped down onto one of the kitchen chairs.

"Grab a seat," my dad said.

I sat down next to him.

"Have you contacted Mr. Ling and Mr. Chang yet to give them the news?"

"No," I said. "I have until the end of today to decide."

"Excellent. Your mother and I have been talking. While we've missed you very much, we think it makes sense for you to go to China for a week."

I groaned. "Mom said that last night."

"Well, I'm even more sure of it now," my mom said, cracking some eggs. "It would be a wonderful cultural experience for you. Beyond that, your father and I are both going to be buried with work for the next several weeks. I hate to admit it, but we're not going to see much of each other anyway."

"Unfortunately, it's true," my dad said. "Take today, for example. Your mother and I both have to eat and run this morning. I won't be home until eight, and she has a late dinner meeting with prospective clients. She won't see you until at least ten tonight."

I frowned. "I had enough cultural experiences in San Francisco's Chinatown."

My dad sighed. "What are you going to do for the rest of your summer vacation if you stay home?"

"Hang out with my friends."

"Every single day?" my mom asked. "That seems unlikely. You do realize that you'd see them every day in China, though."

"It's not even the same thing. Here it would be us just hanging out and stuff. Over there, we'd be training and racing. That's work."

My mom came over to the table. She served the food and sat down with us. Everything looked phenomenal. Breakfast had always been my favorite meal of the day, and huevos rancheros was easily my favorite dish. My mom had learned how to cook it from our next-door neighbor back in California, a nice woman from Mexico who owned an awesome taco truck. The dish consisted of chili sauce on top of fried eggs, which were on top of a freshly fried corn tortilla. As side dishes, my mom had made refried beans and spicy Mexican rice. Delicious!

We dug into our food, and my dad said, "Your mother told me last night that you saw Raffi at that BMX track outside of San Francisco."

"Yeah," I mumbled between bites. "He moved there with his folks two years ago. He gets free gear from a bunch of BMX companies now. I'm sort of jealous."

"Are you interested in racing again?"

"Not really, but I am thinking about buying a BMX bike."

"Are there any BMX tracks around here?" my mom asked.

"I did some surfing on my tablet at the airport. There is a track at a place called Indy Cycloplex. It's the home of Marian University's BMX team."

"Colleges offer scholarships for BMX?"

"Some do."

"I guess that makes sense," my dad said. "BMX has been an Olympic sport for a while now. Are there any BMX shops in town?"

"There's a bike shop in Broad Ripple called Bicycle Exchange that looks pretty sweet. One of the owners still races BMX; the other builds custom bike frames like Hú Dié."

"We'll have to check it out in a few weeks."

"A few *weeks*?" I said. "I was hoping we could go there in the next few days. I want to get a BMX bike so that I can do street tricks around the neighborhood like I used to do in California. It would keep me occupied when my friends can't hang out."

My dad shook his head as he wolfed down the last of his breakfast. "Sorry, champ, I just don't have the time. A big trial has just begun. It's going to be a long one."

I turned to my mother.

She frowned. I noticed that she'd already finished her breakfast, too. "Same story here, I'm afraid," she said.

"Didn't Mr. Ling say something about you possibly riding BMX in China?"

"Not the same thing," I said. "Not even close."

"How do you know?"

"I guess I don't know, but I'd have to stay there longer than one week to do BMX. The one-week trip is only to race road bikes."

"Well, perhaps you should consider staying longer," my dad said. "It's highly probable that you'll never get another chance like this again."

"That's what everyone keeps saying."

My dad stood. "Well, I've learned that if *everyone* tells me the same thing, perhaps I should listen. Give it some more thought, Jake. We can discuss it further tonight, if you'd like. Right now, I've got to run."

My mom stood, too. "I've got to leave as well. Your father and I will support whatever decision you make. We just don't want you to regret not pursuing this opportunity."

"Thanks," I said, shoveling a forkful of refried beans into my mouth. I was only half done with my breakfast.

"Pizza tonight?" my dad asked as he headed for the main hallway.

"Sure," I muttered. "Text me when you leave the office. I'll order and you can pick it up."

"Sounds good," my dad said as he disappeared around the corner. "See you!"

"See you," I replied.

My mom grabbed my dad's dirty dish along with hers.

"I'll get those, Mom," I said. "Don't worry about them."

My mom put the plates back onto the table. "You are a dear," she said, kissing me on the cheek. "Maybe tonight you can tell me more about your trip."

"Okay."

"Have a nice day, baby."

"You too."

I finished breakfast and did the dishes, then plopped down onto the couch in the living room. I thought about trying to get some more sleep, but I was way too restless. I flipped though a couple hundred television channels but didn't see anything interesting.

I checked the time.

Ten a.m.

I wondered if Ryan was awake. He'd slept through the entire flight, so maybe he was. I picked up my cell phone and called him.

It went right to voicemail.

I couldn't remember whether he'd lost his cell phone during our adventures in California, so I called his home number. His mom answered on the first ring.

"Hello, Jake?"

"Yeah, hi, Mrs. Vanderhausen," I said. "It's me."

"Are you okay? Is something wrong?"

"No, not at all. I was just wondering if Ryan was awake."

"I'm sorry," she said. "He ate a huge bacon-and-egg breakfast and went right back to sleep. He'll probably be out for a few more hours."

"That's okay. Can you have him give me a call when he wakes up?"

"Sure, except I can tell you now that he won't have time to hang out with you today, if that's what you're hoping for. I don't mean to sound greedy, but I want some alone time with him."

"I understand," I said. "He can just call me tomorrow or whenever."

"Tomorrow or whenever?" she repeated. "What about China? Have you decided that you don't want to go? Back at the airport, you said that you were considering it."

"I did consider it. On the plane, I more or less decided that I'll take a pass. I want to just chill out until school starts back up. Life has been pretty hectic lately."

"It certainly has, but that's all behind you now, Jake. You should think about your future. Hok called me half an hour ago. She was up all night, talking with well-connected friends in China. I asked her to look into Mr. Chang, and it turns out that he is the real deal. I know you're concerned about living in a foreign country for a year or more, and I understand that. However, spending just one week to try to make a splash is another story altogether. This is a major opportunity. I don't think you should pass it up."

I groaned. "You sound just like my parents."

"They are very intelligent people."

"I know they are, but they don't have to do all the traveling and training and stuff."

"Give it some more thought, please," Ryan's mom said. "You'll have your entire life to ride for fun. The window of opportunity for racing is very narrow. You need to jump through it while you can. You have a gift, Jake. Use it."

"I hear you loud and clear, Mrs. Vanderhausen. Thank

you for the advice. I mean it. I know you've spent a lot of time in the bike racing world. If I decide to go, you'll be the first to know besides my parents."

"I appreciate that. Now go take a nap. Your body thinks it's seven a.m. instead of ten because of the time change from California. By this evening, you'll have run out of gas."

"I'll try," I said.

"All right, then. Goodbye, Jake."

"Goodbye."

I hung up the phone. So much for hanging out with Ryan.

I dialed Phoenix's home number.

It was busy.

I shook my head. Phoenix didn't own a cell phone. Apparently, his landline didn't have call waiting, either. It shouldn't have surprised me. He and his grandfather didn't have much money. Many of the kids at our school were rich, and a lot of them ripped on Phoenix behind his back for being poor. I wouldn't call him poor, but he did wear his clothes a little longer than most people would, and the mountain bike he rode to school was pretty rough. I actually respected him for it, though. Phoenix rode the worst bike in every mountain bike race he ever entered, and unless he crashed, he always won.

I dialed his number again.

Still busy.

Not cool. I didn't feel like waiting around anymore.

Phoenix only lived a mile or so from me. If I jumped on my bike, I could be at his front door in less than five minutes. If I got there and he was too busy or asleep or something, I could just ride back home. Or maybe Hú Dié was awake and could hang out. She was staying with him.

I turned off the TV, grabbed my mountain bike helmet, and headed for the garage.

It took me only four minutes to reach the end of Phoenix's street, but I paused before going any farther. I began to wonder if I was making a mistake. I knew where he lived, of course, but I'd never actually been to his house.

Phoenix's grandfather was really weird about having people over. I used to think it was because he was ashamed that their house was old or a lot smaller than most people's or something. I now understood that it was because he had dragon bone stashed away there. Ever since thieves broke into their house to steal it, though, Phoenix's grandfather had changed his attitude and begun to let people who knew about dragon bone visit.

Even so, I hoped it wouldn't be a big deal that I just showed up out of the blue. I took a deep breath and continued on.

Phoenix's driveway was long and winding, a gravel path between dense trees. The trees opened to a wide, grassy area, and in the middle of the grass was a small, tidy house. I couldn't see through the thick trees beyond the house, but I knew that the White River was back there. Our huge house was cool and all, but I'd switch houses with Phoenix in a second. It was sweet.

The garage door was closed, and Phoenix's grandfather's

old pickup truck was parked in front of it. Behind the pickup was another car that I was pretty sure belonged to Phoenix's uncle Tí.

I coasted toward the house, thinking about how much fun I'd have doing tricks on a BMX bike in all this soft grass, when I heard someone shouting inside. It was Hú Dié. Phoenix sounded like he was trying to calm her down.

I eased closer to an open window, feeling like the sneaky jackal Hok had labeled me back in Chinatown.

"Why can you not do this for me?" Hú Dié asked.

"Because it's not mine to give," Phoenix replied.

"Oh, so you can take it, but you cannot give it?"

"I took it from my grandfather, so the only person I can give it to is him."

"I will ask him, then."

"No! He'll kill me if he ever finds out that I took it."

"That makes no sense. You plan to give it back to him anyway."

"In ten years," Phoenix said. "I'll have figured out what to say to him by then."

"I cannot believe this," Hú Dié said. "What am I going to do?"

"What about Hok?"

"She said that she will consult with PawPaw in China about alternatives, but it will take time. There may not be much time left. That is why I have come to you."

"I don't know," Phoenix said. "Even if I could help you, how would I do it? It's not like I can travel that far without my grandfather or Uncle Tí coming along. I'm going to have to think about this."

"Argh!" Hú Dié shouted. "Just forget it!"

I heard a door slam.

Five seconds later, she came tearing around the back of the house, riding a mountain bike while strapping on her helmet. She was nearly on top of me before she even realized that I was there. She skidded to a stop beside me and I saw that she was sobbing. Huge, sloppy tears poured down her face.

"What's wrong?" I asked.

Hú Dié sniffled and blinked, trying to stem the flood. "It is my mother. She has taken a turn for the worse. I must return to China today. Phoenix's uncle Tí is taking me to the airport in two hours."

"Oh, no!" I said. "I'm so sorry!"

She nodded. "Thank you."

"Where are you going?"

"I . . . do not know. I need to get out of that house for the moment."

"Why?"

"Phoenix. He can be impossible sometimes."

"You don't have to tell me that. Is there anything I can do?"

"Yes," she said, wiping her face. "Ride with me, Jake."

STAGE TWO

A bicycle ride is a flight from sadness.
—James E. Starrs

I chased after Hú Dié as she rocketed along Phoenix's long, serpentine driveway at breakneck speed. She rode as if she were being chased by demons.

Maybe she was. I just hoped she could ride fast enough to escape them, at least for a little while.

The gravel drive was at least a quarter of a mile long, and she reached the end of it several bike lengths ahead of me. She kidded to a stop, and a cloud of dust rose around her, sticking to her now-sweaty face and bare arms. Tears still streamed from her eyes, leaving muddy trails across her cheeks. She was breathing hard, but the intensity of her effort seemed to already be helping her feel better. I was gasping for breath myself, wondering if I'd be able to survive many more sprints like that.

"Where . . . to?" I huffed.

"Town Run . . . Trail Park . . . I suppose," she replied

between huffs and sniffles. "That is the only place . . . I know. I have only traveled there by car, though."

"Your call," I said. "It will take . . . thirty minutes to ride there and back if we hammer, plus another thirty to . . . do the whole trail loop at top speed."

Hú Dié frowned. "I do not have an hour. Maybe I should just . . . go back to Phoenix's house."

"No," I said. "I know a place. We'll be back in half an hour. Forty-five minutes, tops. We'll have the place to ourselves."

Hú Dié half smiled. "That sounds perfect. I knew I could count on you, Jake. Thank you."

"No problem. Follow me."

The place I had in mind was an old gravel pit that was surrounded by trees. Nobody ever went back there. It was Phoenix's secret getaway place, and he showed it to me last year. I felt okay taking Hú Dié there, though. Her being upset was Phoenix's fault.

I pedaled hard to the end of Phoenix's street, then turned and bombed along a wide asphalt pedestrian path. Hú Dié kept pace with me, riding next to me instead of in my slipstream like we'd trained to do on road bikes. Whether she did it because she wanted the company or because she wanted to suffer as much as possible, I wasn't sure. All I knew was that I ran out of gears and reached my maximum possible speed, and she was still next to me, keeping pace.

The girl could *ride*.

"Turn . . . here," I gasped, and I tapped my brakes. I cut my wheel onto a narrow deer run that was barely visible through thick ivy that hung from a wall of towering trees.

Hú Dié expertly eased behind me, following along the game trail. Shaped by animals, it meandered wildly on its path to the river. It hadn't been groomed, and trees hadn't been cut down to keep the trail moving in a straight line. Rocks, roots, and potholes jarred my bones, while low-hanging branches nearly took my head off.

In other words, it was awesome.

Hú Dié and I murdered that trail. By the time we snaked between the small lakes and reached the river, we were both covered head to toe in rotting leaves and rich black humus. We were so out of breath, neither one of us could speak for a full two minutes. I pulled my cell phone out of one of my cargo shorts pockets and checked the time. We'd only been gone twelve minutes, but it felt like twelve hours.

Hú Dié leaned toward me and looked at my phone.

"It looks like we have a little time to enjoy the view before heading back," she said, turning to face the river. "It is so beautiful here."

She was right. The river was close to a hundred feet wide at this point, and it was unusually clear. There wasn't a house or car in sight, and the air smelled fresh and clean. Songbirds chirped all around us while a magnificent great blue heron hunted the shallows on the opposite side of the river. It was picture-perfect.

Hú Dié turned to me. "Thank you for bringing me here, Jake. I will always remember this place. I will always remember you, too."

I felt my eyebrows rise in surprise. "What do you mean? You'd better remember me! It's not like we're never going to talk again." I paused. "I mean, you're going to keep in touch, right?"

She shrugged. "I will try. You never know how these things will turn out, though. Nothing ever seems to work out the way I would like." Tears welled up in her eyes once more.

Man, she was low. I felt so bad for her. "Is there anything you'd like to talk about?" I asked.

"Such as?"

"I don't know. When I'm bummed, it usually makes me feel better if I talk about it."

"That is not how I was raised," she said. "I was taught not to burden others with my emotions. It is like this for many Chinese."

"Well, you're not in China right now. Let loose. What have you got to lose?"

"Your friendship, for one. I may have already lost a friend today, possibly more."

"Who? Phoenix?"

"Yes," she said. "Phoenix, and maybe his grandfather, as well as his uncle Tí. Perhaps Hok in San Francisco, too, if Phoenix tells her what I was asking for."

"Why?"

Hú Dié sighed. "I suppose Phoenix will tell you once I leave, anyway. I asked his grandfather for some dragon bone to give to my mother. When he declined, I called Hok. She declined as well."

"Are you sure dragon bone will help your mother? She has ALS, right?"

"Yes. It is a disease of the nerve cells in her brain and

spinal cord. Those are exactly the cells that I believe dragon bone connects with and enhances or repairs. She has lost nearly all control of her muscles, but her mind is still as keen as ever. It is a horrible disease."

I couldn't even begin to imagine what Hú Dié's mother must have been going through. "I am so sorry," I said. "I wish I could help you somehow."

She locked eyes with me. "Do you?" she asked. "Do you *really*, Jake?"

"Of course, I—" Hú Dié was looking at me funny. "Wait a minute," I said. "What do you want me to do?"

She didn't answer. She just stared at me.

And then I knew what she wanted.

"No way!" I said, putting one foot atop a pedal to leave. "Hok may have called me a sneaky jackal, but I will *not* steal from Phoenix's grandfather or anybody else."

"No, no, no, Jake!" Hú Dié said in a rush. "I would never ask you to steal anything from anyone! Please, do not leave yet."

"Tell me what you want, then."

She bit her lower lip. "If I tell you a secret, do you promise not to share it with anyone?"

"Now you sound just like Phoenix, making everyone keep quiet about his family's secrets."

She suddenly scowled, and for a second I thought she was going to punch me. But then she lightened up. "Maybe you are correct, for this is his secret, too."

I took my foot off of the pedal. "Fine, tell me."

"Phoenix and I hid some dragon bone in case of an

emergency. Nobody else knows about it. Not his grandfather. Not Hok. Nobody."

"Great," I said. "Except me now."

"Yes, except you now."

"And you want me to get it for you?"

"If you would be willing."

"Why don't you get it yourself?"

"I cannot," she said. "There is not enough time."

I shook my head. She was right.

"Why me?" I asked. "Shouldn't you ask Phoenix to get it for you? Wait, that's what you guys were arguing about in the house, isn't it?"

"You overheard us?"

"Um, kind of."

She frowned. "Yes, that is what we were discussing. Phoenix said that he needs to think about it more, but my mother may not be able to wait any longer."

"I heard him say something about ten years," I said. "What was that all about?"

"Phoenix's grandfather's supply of dragon bone is scheduled to run out after that time. Phoenix plans to retrieve the extra supply and offer it to his grandfather as an option to extend his life beyond those ten years."

I blinked. "Phoenix's grandfather is *scheduled* to die in ten years?"

"Yes. Phoenix's grandfather came up with that plan. He wants to be finished with dragon bone, but he does not want to die until Phoenix is grown up. He ordered Phoenix to send all of the remaining dragon bone he had to a woman named PawPaw, in China, as well as a man named Grandmaster

Long, who is also in China. Those two individuals are both dragon bone users, and they each now have enough dragon bone to last them more than one hundred years. I believe Hok possesses roughly the same amount through her own sources."

"I remember Phoenix telling me some of this in California," I said, "but he didn't say anything about how much dragon bone was left, or who had what amounts. This is insane! Phoenix's grandfather is going to die in ten years, while three other ancient people live a hundred more years? And even though Hok has a hundred-year supply, she won't give you *any* to help your mother?"

"That is correct," Hú Dié said with a sniffle. "Hok and Phoenix's grandfather do not want another person having to take it the rest of his or her life. Hok did promise to try to find alternative Chinese herbal treatments for my mother. She is going to ask for PawPaw's help, too."

"Why can't one of them give your mother dragon bone for a short time, and then stop? Maybe it will heal her. That's how people used to use dragon bone. Ryan took it for a while and then he stopped by taking that antidote Hok made. He's fine."

"I asked that, too. Hok said that Ryan was healthy to begin with, whereas my mother is not. Hok believes that once my mother begins taking dragon bone, she will need to take it forever, just like Hok, Phoenix's grandfather, PawPaw, and Grandmaster Long. Hok believes the antidote would kill my mother because the dragon bone would become too much a part of her. For the same reason, Hok will not take the antidote, nor give it to any of the other ancient individuals, because she believes it would kill them, too."

"No wonder you're super upset," I said. "How much did you and Phoenix hide?"

"Fifteen years' worth."

I rolled my eyes. "Phoenix hid that much—with your help—but he won't even share part of it with you?"

Hú Dié shrugged. "He said that he needed to think about it more."

"Where is it?"

"Pine Loop Mountain Bike Trail in Brown County State Park."

I thought about that for a moment and realized something. "The race we did there," I said, "the one you won and Phoenix came in last because he wrecked—he didn't really wreck, did he?"

"No, he did not," Hú Dié said. "He only pretended to crash in order to buy himself enough time to hide the dragon bone."

"But . . . how?"

"Do you remember us both wearing those large hydration backpacks?"

"Yeah," I said. "I thought it was a little odd for you to have them for such a short race."

"I had a folding shovel in mine," Hú Dié said. "I threw him my pack a few minutes into the race when we were ahead of everyone else, and he threw it back to me at the end. He slid down a very tall hill with his bike in order to get near the finish line ahead of everyone else. He only made it look like he wrecked at that late point in the race."

"So the dragon bone is buried near the *beginning* of Pine Loop?"

"Yes."

"Where, exactly?"

Hú Dié locked eyes with me again. "If I tell you, will you help me?"

I rubbed my sweaty forehead beneath my helmet. "I may hate myself later, but yeah, since Phoenix can't seem to make up his mind, I'll do it. Tell me everything I need to know."

Hú Dié was so happy, I thought she was going to kiss me. She didn't, though. Instead, she punched me in the arm.

Hard.

"Ouch!" I yelped. "What did you do that for?"

"I am too full of excitement!" she said. "I need to release some energy."

I shook my head. "You can release that energy on our sprint back to Phoenix's house." I checked the time on my phone again. "We've been gone almost twenty-five minutes."

"I can spare another five minutes," Hú Dié said. "I promise I will not hit you again. I need to give you clues about how to find the dragon bone."

"Clues?"

"Phoenix would not tell me exactly where it is, but you can figure it out. You are clever—like a jackal."

I smirked.

Hú Dié continued. "Phoenix pulled off the trail right

before a short, steep climb that was really dusty and covered with small rocks. It is the first place most people get off of their bikes on Pine Loop."

"I know the spot," I said. "There are a bunch of tall ferns right there, before the climb."

"Yes! That is where Phoenix hid his bike. You have an amazing memory."

"It comes with being a jackal. What else?"

"The shovel in my backpack," Hú Dié said. "It was clean when I tossed the pack to him, but kind of dirty when he returned it. He had wiped most of the dirt off before putting it back into the pack, but it still smelled really bad."

"You mean, like garbage?"

"It smelled worse than garbage. Phoenix's shoes stunk, too. When we got home, I found a tiny piece of what appeared to be a mushroom inside the backpack that was not there before. I did some surfing on the Internet, and I believe that Phoenix buried or hid the dragon bone within a patch of stinkhorn mushrooms."

"*Buried or hid?* He brought back a dirty shovel. He buried it."

"Maybe," she said, "or maybe just half buried. He accidentally mentioned something about a tiny cave. If you can find a rock outcropping near a patch of stinkhorn mushrooms somewhere near those ferns, I believe you will find the dragon bone. It will be in a silk drawstring bag."

"Supposing I find it, how am I supposed to get it to you? Mail it?"

"No. Phoenix mailed large quantities to PawPaw and Grandmaster Long, but PawPaw arranged everything. We cannot ask her to get involved with this. She would say something to Hok and Phoenix's grandfather, and I would be out of luck—and you would be out of a lot of money. You might even get in trouble for mailing it. Even though dragon bone is a natural substance, I do not know the laws about shipping medicinal herbs out of this country."

"What am I supposed to do, then?"

Hú Dié sniffled and wiped her eyes. She gave me a pleading look.

I braced myself.

"You could bring it to China," she said.

I groaned. I had a feeling she was leading up to this. "You want me to call Ling and accept Mr. Chang's offer to try China for one week."

"I really do think you would enjoy China. Honest."

"I don't know, Hú Dié. Riding in China is one thing, but smuggling dragon bone is another. My parents are lawyers. What you're talking about could be some kind of serious offense. How would I even get it through security and customs and all that?"

"Phoenix once hid dragon bone inside a container of protein powder he had emptied out. It fooled the police in Texas."

"Are you even listening to yourself?" I asked. "This all sounds so crazy."

Hú Dié began to sob again. "You are right, Jake. It is crazy. I just do not have anyone else to turn to. I am sorry that I bothered you with it." She turned away from me, her back heaving from the effort of crying.

I felt like a jerk. I couldn't stand to see her like this. It sounded like dragon bone was probably Hú Dié's mother's only shot at staying alive.

Before even I realized what I was doing, I heard myself say, "I guess I could do it, Hú Dié. At least traveling to China would give me some more time to hang out with you."

Hú Dié turned back to me, and her dirt-streaked, soaking-wet face lit up like the sun. "Are you certain?"

"Yes, I'm certain."

"You are the best ever! I cannot wait to show you my hometown of Kaifeng."

I began to smile, but then it quickly faded. "Kaifeng? What about Shanghai? You'd still race there on Saturday if I came to China, right?"

"I hope so. It depends on my mother's condition, though."

"I understand," I said. "I guess I'm going to have to figure out a way to bum a ride to Brown County tomorrow."

Hú Dié looked concerned. "No, Jake. You should try to retrieve it today. You are supposed to contact Ling and Mr. Chang by tonight if you want to accept their offer, and they will probably want to fly you out tomorrow. The race is on Saturday, and it's already Monday."

"But how can I possibly get to Brown County today?" I asked. "My parents are both tied up until tonight."

"Back home, I would just call a taxi."

I thought about it for a second. "That could work. Or maybe a private shuttle car like my mom and dad take home from the airport when they have to go out of town."

"I have about fifty dollars left that I can give you."

"Don't worry about it," I said. "I don't want your money."

"I will think of some way to repay you," Hú Dié said. "You will see."

"You don't have to—"

Someone suddenly shouted, *"There you guys are!"*

It was Phoenix.

He rolled up to us atop his mountain bike, and he didn't look happy. "I should have known you'd bring her here, Jake. What were you two talking about?"

I swallowed hard. "Nothing, I—"

"Jake was just telling me that he is going to accept Mr. Chang's offer to try riding in China for a week!" Hú Dié said without missing a beat. "Is that not exciting?" She wiped more tears from her face.

Phoenix eyed her suspiciously. "Then why are you crying?"

"Because I am *happy*," Hú Dié said. "It does not erase all of my sadness, of course, but it makes me feel better. Are you not excited?"

"No. I'm leery." Phoenix turned to me. "Is it true?"

"You bet, bro!" I said, trying my best to sound stoked. "I want us to keep hanging out together. Hú Dié has to go back home, so, you know, the only way for us to chill is for all of us to go there."

Phoenix still didn't look convinced. "Hú Dié is going to race?"

"Yes," she answered. "I will talk with Ling and Mr. Chang about me spending a few days with my mother, then joining you in Shanghai. If I need to hurry back home for some reason, Shanghai is only a few hours away from Kaifeng by bullet train."

"Bullet train?" Phoenix said, smiling a little. "I've always wanted to ride on one of those."

"There is a bullet train that runs from Shanghai airport to downtown Shanghai," Hú Dié said. "You will probably ride it after you land."

Phoenix's smile grew. "This sounds legit."

"It is," I said. "We're going to China."

"Rock and roll!" Phoenix said. "Have you told Ryan yet?"

"Nope."

Phoenix spun his bike around, aiming it up the narrow game trail. "Well, what are you waiting for? Let's get back to my house and call him!"

9

We made it back to Phoenix's house even faster than Hú Dié and I had ridden to the river, which was a good thing. She and I had spent too much time talking, and she still needed to shower and pack.

Hú Dié kicked off her shoes and raced into the house, while Phoenix and I remained outside on the back porch. It wasn't that I was afraid to go inside; it's just that I was filthy. His house may have been small, but it looked neat as a pin.

Phoenix's grandfather and Uncle Tí came out to greet me, and I tried to not react to what I saw. Phoenix's grandfather had gone through some rough times over the past few months, and it showed. His tall, slender body was now hunched and kind of shaky; and his previously long, thick hair had become wispy and thin. Phoenix's uncle Tí looked the same way he'd always looked, like a healthy, middle-aged Chinese physician with a receding hairline.

I took off my helmet and shook my hair out.

"Wow," Uncle Tí said. "I wish I had hair like that."

I laughed. "Hi," I said.

"Hello, Jake."

Phoenix's grandfather nodded his hello. He wasn't much of a talker. I nodded back.

Uncle Tí looked at the soil and leaves stuck to my legs, and he grinned. "It was kind of you to take Hú Dié for a quick ride. It clearly improved her mood."

"No big deal. It helps me all the time, but I didn't plan it. I actually came here to talk to Phoenix."

"Yeah," Phoenix said. "Guess what?"

"Jake has decided to conquer China, after all?" Uncle Tí asked.

"Yes!" Phoenix said.

"Congratulations to both of you," Uncle Tí said. "Ryan, too."

"Thanks," I said. "I wouldn't have won that race in California if it wasn't for them pulling me."

"Does Ryan know about your decision?"

"Not yet. I'm about to call him. I actually need to call my folks first, though. I haven't even told them my decision yet."

"Don't let us get in your way," Uncle Tí said. "We just came out to say hello."

"Thanks," I said.

Phoenix's grandfather and Uncle Tí headed back into the house.

I pulled my cell phone out of my pocket and saw that it wasn't quite noon. Perfect. Lunchtime was about the only time you could catch my mother on a workday. I called her cell.

She picked right up.

"Jake?" my mother said.

"Hi, Mom," I said. "I know you're busy, so I won't keep you. I just need to ask you something."

"Yes?"

"Is it still fine with you and Dad if I go to China for one week?"

"Of course!" she said. "If I recall correctly, I was the one who first encouraged you to do it."

"I know," I said. "I just wanted to make sure. I'm at Phoenix's house now, and—"

"And you didn't call or text me to let me know that you were leaving the house?" she interrupted.

"Oops," I said. "Sorry. I forgot. I was just so excited to—"

"Never mind," she said. "We can talk about it later at home. We'll have to discuss a few rules for China, too. Let me know if you go anywhere else today."

"Will do," I said. "Can I call Dad and tell him the news?"

"No. He's in court today, remember? No cell phones allowed. You'll see him tonight, before you see me, though."

"Oh, yeah. Good luck with your dinner meeting tonight."

"Thank you. I'm looking forward to seeing you when I get home, baby."

"Same here. Bye, Mom."

"Bye."

I turned to Phoenix. "Looks like we're in."

He grinned. "Sweet."

I called Ryan's house next.

Ryan's mom answered. "Hello, Jake. Ryan is still asleep."

"That's okay," I said. "I was actually calling to talk to you."

"Oh?"

"I've decided to go to China."

She squealed with delight. "Oh! That is wonderful news! I'll let Ryan know as soon as he wakes up! Is there anything we need to do?"

"I'm sure there is, but I don't know what yet. I still have to call Mr. Chang and his translator and helper, Ling, to let them know."

"I'm assuming you're only planning to go for one week," she said.

"Yeah."

"Good choice. Try it out first, then decide what's best for you. I'm proud of you for giving it a shot."

"Thank you, Mrs. Vanderhausen."

"You'd better run along and make that call now. I'll have Ryan give you a ring the moment he rolls out of bed."

"Cool. Bye."

"Goodbye."

I hung up and looked at Phoenix. "Ryan is asleep."

"It figures," Phoenix said.

"Time to call Ling," I said.

I fished around in one of the pockets of my cargo shorts and pulled out Ling's business card. There was a phone number with a weird pattern of digits printed on the front, but a normal-looking telephone number with area code was handwritten on the back. I flashed the handwritten number at Phoenix.

"It's a San Francisco number," I said. "I remember seeing that area code printed on stuff out there."

"You and your crazy memory," Phoenix said. "Ling probably rented a cell phone in San Francisco. It's noon here, so that's nine a.m. in California now. You should call him."

I nodded and dialed the digits. Someone answered right away.

"Hello?"

It was Ling. I recognized his voice.

"Hi," I said. "This is Jake, from Indiana."

"Jake!" Ling said. "How are you?"

"Real good. Is Mr. Chang with you?"

"He is."

"Great," I said, and took a deep breath. "I just wanted to let you both know that I would like to come to China for one week, if that is still an option."

"Wonderful!" Ling said. "Of course it is still an option. We were just talking about you. I was so hoping you would call today. I've already made preliminary arrangements to host you and your friends. I had a hunch you would want to do it for a week. Just a moment. Let me tell Mr. Chang."

I heard Ling begin to talk in Chinese, then Mr. Chang's deep-voiced reply. Mr. Chang sounded pleased. It made me feel good.

Ling came back on the line. "Mr. Chang wishes to congratulate you on your excellent decision. Have you spoken with your friends yet?"

"All of them except Ryan, but I just got off the phone with his mother. Everyone's really excited."

"Glad to hear it. I will need to speak with their parents

or guardians as soon as possible. I'll need to speak with your parents, too."

"Sure. I'll give everyone your number and ask their folks to call you as soon as possible. When do you want us to come?"

"I can have you on a plane tomorrow if your parents sign the visa documentation and other forms in time."

"Whoa," I said.

"Mr. Chang is not one to dillydally. Our graphic designer has already begun mocking up advertisements with images of you four from the recent race. Your parents will need to sign releases for these things, too."

"My parents won't be able to get back to you until late tonight. I hope that won't be a problem."

"That's fine. I can still make most of the arrangements now."

"I should probably let you know, too, that Hú Dié is flying home to Kaifeng in a couple hours. Her mom has a . . . condition. I can have her call you as soon as I hang up."

"I'd appreciate that," Ling said. "Do you have questions?"

"Not really," I said. "I know how training camps work. I'm guessing this is pretty much the same thing, except with people taking our picture a bunch and maybe some interviews."

"Exactly," Ling said. "You won't be living in a cramped dormitory like most training cyclists, though. You'll be staying in a beautiful apartment complex that's centered in a Western-style area of Shanghai. It's brand-new, and it's where most American visitors prefer to stay. Many people speak English there. You'll feel right at home."

"Awesome," I said.

"Feel free to call me anytime if you or your friends have questions," Ling said, "and you can pack light for this trip. We'll provide you with uniforms for riding and tracksuits and shorts for relaxing. We'll also feed you and provide all of your bicycles and gear. Just bring spending money for gifts and souvenirs. With luck, though, you won't even need that because you won't want to leave!"

"We'll see," I said.

"You and I can talk more tonight when your parents call me," Ling said.

"Yep," I said. "Talk to you later."

"Goodbye, Jake."

I hung up.

Phoenix said, "This is really going to happen."

"Sure enough, bro," I replied. "You got a pen and some paper? I need to give you Ling's digits."

"Be right back." Phoenix ran into the house and came out seconds later with a pencil and stack of sticky notes.

Hú Dié poked her head out of the back door. She was wearing clean clothes, and her long black hair was wrapped in a towel. I walked over and handed her a sticky note with Ling's number. "I told Ling that you were flying home in a few hours because of your mom. I didn't give him any details. He needs you to call him as soon as possible."

She nodded.

I handed Phoenix a sticky note with Ling's number as well as the pencil and remaining sticky notes.

"I've got to jet," I said. "Lots of stuff to do before we leave."

Hú Dié smiled at me. She knew what I really meant. "I am very glad that you decided to do this, Jake," she said. "I will see you in China."

"Yeah," I said, "see you in China."

It felt like we probably should have hugged or something, but I was covered in trail goo and she was sparkling clean. Plus, it seemed kind of awkward with Phoenix there. Instead, I just nodded to her, and she nodded back.

Hú Dié turned and went back into the house, and I headed for my bike.

Phoenix gave me a wave. "See you, bro."

I waved back. "Yeah, see you, bro."

I pedaled away, wondering how much longer Phoenix and I would actually be bros. Once he found out about my little trip to Pine Loop in Brown County State Park, he might never speak to me again.

I frowned and began to hammer. I might as well get this over with. It was well past noon now, and my dad would be home around eight p.m. It was a two-hour round trip to the state park, plus it would take about an hour for me to line up transportation and get my gear ready. That left me about four and a half or five hours to find the dragon bone.

Not a problem for a clever, sneaky—and fast—*jackal* like me.

I got home and took a quick shower to get most of the trail crud off of me, then jumped online to check the status of the Pine Loop trail in Brown County State Park. Trails closed all the time, for reasons like flooding or trail rebuilding, but I was in luck. Pine Loop was open. Better still, it was open under a yellow cautionary status, which meant "ride at your own risk." Most riders would stay off the trail under these conditions. I might have the place to myself.

Next, I found the website for a local taxi company and called them on my cell phone. I lowered my voice to sound as much like an adult as possible and told the dispatcher what I needed for "my son." She said that a taxi with a running meter would be ridiculously expensive. Also, their taxis didn't have bike racks. However, they were running a week-day special on their limousines, which had trailer hitches to which they could attach one of their bike racks. They could have a limo with a bike rack at my doorstep in twenty minutes for "only" $300.

That was quite a bit of money, but I'm almost embarrassed to say that I had more than that in my sock drawer. My parents made a very good living, and it trickled down to me in the form of my allowance and a prepaid credit card that I used for things like food when they were both gone. I'd never been in a limo before, and it seemed like it would be cool. Besides, I had no idea how else I'd get to the trail.

I booked the limo.

I made arrangements for the driver to meet me somewhere other than my doorstep. No need to alert the neighbors to my plans if I wasn't even going to tell my folks. I reserved it with my credit card, but told them I would pay cash at the end of the trip. That way my parents wouldn't see the charge if they ever went looking.

I put my credit card back into my wallet along with all the cash from my sock drawer, and I headed out to the garage to grab a few essentials. I was already wearing a clean pair of mountain biking shorts that had two large cargo pockets, but the short-sleeved mountain biking shirt I was wearing didn't have any pockets, so I grabbed my empty hydration backpack.

Sizing up the pack, I scanned the wall of garden tools. None of the tools would fit into the pockets of my shorts, but there was a miniature rake that would fit in the pack. The rake had three pointy tines, so I'd have to be careful to keep them positioned away from the hydration bladder. I would have preferred to pull the bladder out, but I'd be gone for hours and I'd definitely need something to drink.

I put the rake into the backpack and gathered up my helmet, riding shoes, riding gloves, and sunglasses, and took everything out to the driveway, along with my mountain bike. I ran back into the house to fill the hydration bladder with water, and I stuffed one of my pockets with energy bars. Then I shoved my wallet and cell phone into my other pocket and locked up the house.

I geared up in the driveway and raced out of my neighborhood with my heart beating faster than it should. I tried not to think about all the rules I was breaking. My mom had already given me a hard time about not telling her that I'd gone to Phoenix's house. If she found out about the limo, there would be no way that she'd allow me to go to China. I might successfully find the dragon bone and bring it home, but not have a way to get it to Hú Dié. Whatever happened, I needed to make sure that I was home before either of my parents.

I reached the parking lot of a large grocery store as a long black limousine swung into it. I smiled despite my nervousness. The limo looked sweet. The driver parked, and I pulled up beside his window. He wasn't all that old, maybe a college student, and was wearing a suit and tie. He tried to ignore me, but I banged on the window and pointed to the bike rack attached to the back of the limo. His eyebrows raised, and he lowered his window.

"You've got to be kidding me," he said.

"No joke," I said, taking off my helmet and sunglasses.

"You're my ride. You want me to put my bike on the rack? Or should you do it?"

The driver frowned. "Just a minute. I was told that I was driving a kid to go mountain biking, but I figured there would be, you know, a parent or adult along for the ride."

"Nope, just me."

"I'm not sure this is cool. I need to check into it." He picked up a cell phone.

"My dad booked the limo for me," I said hurriedly. "He's a lawyer. You want to check with him?"

"A lawyer?" the driver said, putting the phone back down. "Well, if he doesn't have a problem with it, we're good. I'll get your bike, kid. You get in the back." He opened his door and got out.

I did my best to contain my relief, glad that he didn't call my bluff. I got off of my bike and handed it over, then climbed into the rear of the limo, removing my hydration backpack. I closed the door and glanced around. This was easily the coolest vehicle I'd ever been in. You could only enter the gigantic rear passenger section from one side of the limo because the other side was a massive leather seat that wrapped almost all the way around the perimeter. You could probably fit ten adults back here. There was a small bar stocked with bottled water and soda. There were also two televisions and at least a dozen surround-sound speakers. LED rope lights ringed the ceiling, the lights pulsing to the beat of dance music.

I took off my riding gloves and found the stereo controls. I had begun to flip through the satellite radio stations when the large glass window separating the passenger area from the driver slid down.

"Ready to roll," the driver said. "Your name's Jake, right? At least, that's what they told me."

"Yes," I replied.

"Nice to meet you, Jake. I'm Michael. You okay back there?"

"I'm great. This is pretty sweet."

"It is. The water and soda are yours for the taking. If you need anything else, just bang on the glass."

"Okay."

Michael glanced at a GPS unit set into the dashboard. "I've got us going to Brown County State Park for a couple hours."

"Yeah," I said. "There's a mountain bike trail called Pine Loop."

"Sounds good. Anyplace else?"

"No. Just back home—" I paused. "Er . . . I mean, here."

Michael smirked. "Your folks don't really know that you're doing this, do they? Otherwise, I'd have picked you up in front of your house."

"Um—"

Michael raised a hand. "No need to answer that. I'd rather not know. Just remember this little conversation when it comes time to tip me at the end of the day."

I didn't reply. I'd forgotten about a tip. It looked like I was going to have to give him a big one.

Michael turned away, but then he looked back over his shoulder. "It's a girl, isn't it?"

"Huh?"

"You're going to meet a girl, aren't you? I mean, there aren't any races or anything on a Monday afternoon, right? And you wouldn't just drop three hundred bucks to ride a stupid trail for a couple hours."

I felt my cheeks begin to redden. I *was* taking this trip because of a girl.

Michael smirked. "I knew it! Your secret is safe with me. She isn't getting into the back of this limo, though."

"No worries," I said. "I . . . I mean, *we* are only going to ride the trails."

Michael nodded. "Just watch yourself. Girls are nothing but trouble, believe me." He looked away again, and the window rose back up.

I shook my head. How many lies was I going to tell today?

The limo began to move, and I turned off the radio. I saw a switch for the lights and turned them off, too. I grabbed the television remote and sank into the long plush leather seat. I flipped through a few satellite TV channels, but just like at home, there wasn't anything interesting on.

I yawned and turned off the TV. I was suddenly tired. It seemed the flight from California, my ride with Hú Dié, and the stress over what I was about to do had taken its toll. I lay down and stretched out. The long, heavy vehicle absorbed every trace of road vibrations, making it feel as though I was back home on my living room couch. Two minutes later, I was sound asleep.

"Jake! Wake up!"

I opened my eyes to find that we'd arrived at the state park. I'd slept like a rock the entire drive. I sat up and saw that the window between Michael and me was down. The limo was pulling up to the park's entrance gate.

"I hope you brought some cash, Jake," Michael said.

"Yeah," I groaned, and I fished my wallet out of my pocket.

Michael stopped beside an entry gate and lowered his window.

"Five dollars, please," a park ranger said.

I handed Michael a five-dollar bill, and he gave it to the ranger in exchange for a receipt to tape to the front windshield.

"What's the best way to get to Pine Loop?" Michael asked.

The ranger handed him a map. "It's in here. Very easy. Just stay on this road."

"Thanks," Michael said. He pulled away from the gate and unfolded the map.

I rubbed my eyes.

"Looks easy enough," Michael said.

"Yeah," I replied. "It's not too far from this entrance."

By the time I put on my helmet, sunglasses, and gloves in the back of the limo, Michael was already pulling into the Pine Loop parking lot. I didn't see any other cars. Michael parked, and we both got out. He took my mountain bike off of the rack as I slipped my hydration backpack over my shoulders.

"Here you go," Michael said, handing my bike to me. "I don't see any sign of your honey."

"What?" I asked.

"Your girlfriend."

"Oh." I glanced at the time on my phone. "It's only two forty-five. I'm early."

"Well, take your time. I'm not going anywhere. I'll be waiting inside the limo for you. If I'm asleep in the driver's seat, just knock on the window. I'll have it open at least part-way because it's kind of hot out here. Don't get heatstroke or anything."

"I won't," I said, pointing to the hydration hose clipped near my right shoulder.

Michael nodded and climbed into the driver's seat, and I pedaled across the parking lot to Pine Loop's start/end point.

It was indeed a hot day, but the moment I hit the trail, which was shaded by tall leafy brush, the temperature dropped at least five degrees. It dropped another five degrees once the brushy stretch ended and the trail opened up to huge, widely spaced oak trees.

I inhaled deeply, savoring the rich aromas of the forest. I felt my stress begin to melt away. My oversized mountain bike was designed for this type of trail, and it handled this section as smoothly as the limo had handled the open road.

The view was spectacular, with the trail running up and then down several deep ravines. I'd learned in science class that the glaciers of the last ice age had stopped advancing near Indianapolis, which is where I lived. The land was flat as a pancake there. Here, though, it was very hilly, like Kentucky or Tennessee.

I breezed along the edge of a particularly deep ravine and slowed down. The trail was under a yellow cautionary status, after all, and this stretch contained a few puddles of water. Riding through the puddles would leave ruts on the trail that would then harden and make it miserable for future riders. Worse than that, puddles were slippery. I didn't want to find myself slipping down that nasty drop.

I cleared the stretch along the ravine and wove around a few switchbacks, then over some small hills.

Then I stopped.

Before me was the steep, silty hill that Hú Dié and I had talked about. To one side was a thick cluster of ferns.

I climbed off my bike and pushed it into the ferns. I didn't think anyone would be riding along this trail at this time of day on a weekday, but I wanted to play it safe. I found a big pine tree among the ferns and dropped my bike behind it. I scanned the area with my eyes as well as my nose, searching for signs of stinkhorn mushrooms.

The wind picked up for a second, and I caught a whiff of something rotten. I noted the direction of the breeze and started walking. I hadn't gone more than fifty yards before the stench became almost unbearable. I was on a hillside, and near the top of the hill was a level section of ground that was noticeably darker than the rest of the earth around it. The dark ground was covered with slender mushrooms. Set into the rocky hillside behind the mushrooms were a bunch of pockets that resembled tiny caves.

I grinned. This was the place.

Pulling the collar of my shirt up over my nose, I took the rake from my backpack and headed for the spot where the caves met the stinkhorns. The ground was soft and squishy, and I immediately sank to my ankles. Warm, moist earth oozed into my shoes and seeped through my socks, pooling between my toes.

I cringed. I hadn't been expecting this.

I scanned the line where the flat spot of rich soil met the hillside, but I didn't see any signs that somebody had been here, so I just started whacking away with the little rake. Bits of pungent, gooey earth went airborne, sticking to my legs and arms despite my best efforts to direct the muck away from me.

It took me half an hour of clawing at the rotten ground, but I eventually located Phoenix's hiding spot. He'd blocked off one of the tiny caves with a few rocks and some rancid soil. The blue silk bag appeared to be intact, and I carefully opened it. Inside were several handfuls of gray powder that, even through the mushroom stink, had a strange odor best described as *old*. I remembered Ryan smelling like that whenever he sweated while taking dragon bone. This was it.

I closed the bag and—*SNAP!*—heard a stick break.

I looked back the way I'd come.

A gigantic man was walking toward me. He wore a bicycle helmet and sunglasses and was pushing a huge mountain bike. He stopped at the edge of the mushroom patch, and I noticed that his bare arms were covered with tattoos.

Tattoos of gorillas.

I froze.

"Hello, Jake," DaXing said. "What's in the bag?"

I stared at DaXing, my feet frozen ankle-deep in the squishy ground. This was Gorilla, the guy who'd strangled DuSow to death with his gigantic hands.

I swallowed my urge to scream and asked, "Wh-what's up, DaXing?"

"No time for small talk," he said. "Give me the dragon bone."

"Dragon bone?" I asked. "I don't know what you're talking about. I—"

"Don't make a fool of yourself, Jake. I respect both you and your friends for the manner in which you handled yourselves in California. I do not wish to hurt you. Hand over the dragon bone and be on your way. Forget you ever saw me, and I won't tell anyone that I saw you. I imagine your parents would be quite upset if they were to discover that you rented a limousine so that you could dig up a questionable substance."

"How did you—"

"Lin Tan once told me that he spied on Phoenix racing along this very trail, only to abandon the race. He thought Phoenix might have hidden some dragon bone here. The substance is my ticket back home to China without the authorities catching me. Hand it over."

"I can't," I said, and shoved the blue silk bag into my backpack. I slung the pack onto my back.

DaXing leaned his bike against a tree and took two quick steps toward me onto the rich, gooey soil. His massive bulk made him sink almost up to his knees.

"Argh!" DaXing shouted, and he began to try to pull himself free.

I grabbed the rake and made a break for it, slogging my way to the edge of the mushroom patch. I was half a step from solid ground when DaXing suddenly lunged at me like a linebacker diving at a running back. His thick arms were impossibly long, and he managed to grab hold of my ankle as he went—*SPLAT!*—face-first into the stinkhorns.

I wasn't sure whether the mushrooms were toxic, but he let out a choked wail that suggested something unpleasant had just filled his mouth. I tried to jerk my leg free of his grasp, but he didn't let go. I fell onto my side in the rich soil and kicked at his hand with my free foot. I heard small bones snap each time the metal bracket on the bottom of my riding shoe connected with the slender bones in the back of his hand. He grunted in pain and his other massive hand suddenly shot forward, latching on to my kicking foot.

DaXing began to roll in the rancid patch of soft, moist soil like a crocodile. I had no choice but to roll with him, but

I remembered the rake. The instant we both rolled out of the stinkhorns onto solid ground, I twisted around and sank its three sharp tines into the back of his hand. He howled and let go, and I scrambled to my feet.

DaXing pulled the rake free and managed to hurl it at me with amazing force and accuracy. I turned and ducked, and the rake bounced off the back of my bicycle helmet. The impact knocked me to my knees and I saw stars, but the helmet had taken the brunt of the blow. I was fine.

I jumped to my feet and sprinted away, wanting to run to my bike, but unsure whether I could find it fast enough. DaXing's ride would have to do instead.

I reached the overgrown gorilla's bike and threw a leg over it. I stood on the pedals, but the cleats on my shoes didn't exactly line up with the clips on his pedals. Also, his seat was way too high. I considered dropping the bike and running away, but DaXing roared and got to his feet. He raced toward me, and I instinctively pushed off.

We were on a hill, so I put my faith in gravity. I began to roll quickly, doing my best to keep my feet parallel to the ground and balanced atop the pedal clips. I remembered the general direction of the trail and steered toward it. When I reached the tall ferns, I risked a glance over my shoulder.

DaXing was in hot pursuit. He half bounded, half skidded down the hillside with gigantic strides, gaining on me.

I would have to do better.

I sliced through the ferns, my wheel spokes shredding the foliage like a food processor cutting lettuce. I wove around trees and bounced over rocks, constantly adjusting my feet to keep them in contact with the pedal clips. I couldn't turn the cranks, so I more or less just hung on for the ride until the trail suddenly appeared. There was no point in trying to climb the silty hill, so I headed back toward the parking lot.

I cruised around switchbacks and rolled over several small hills, pumping whenever I could to keep up my speed. I was going pretty fast, but I'd have been flying by now if I was on my own mountain bike.

DaXing shouted something in Chinese and I looked back to see that he was, unbelievably, closer than he'd ever been. He was huffing and puffing like a locomotive, and he showed no sign of slowing. If I didn't pick up more speed, I was doomed.

I rounded a bend, and a lump formed in my throat. I'd reached the stretch where the trail ran along the edge of the park's deepest ravine. The trail had been cut to lay perfectly flat for hundreds of yards with no change in elevation, to minimize the possibility of somebody losing control and tumbling over the edge.

DaXing shouted again, and I realized that it was some kind of triumphant war cry. He was going to catch me.

I couldn't let that happen.

I stared down the ravine, looking for an escape route. It was pointless. The gradient was too steep.

But then I spotted the trunk of a dead tree jutting out of the ravine's slope just a couple feet below the trail. I got an idea. While the ravine was deep, it wasn't all that wide. The branchless trunk spanned nearly three quarters of the ravine's width and angled upward like a ramp. I'd ridden plenty of trails that contained tree trunk "bridges" narrower than this one, and I'd cleared much larger gaps than the one between the end of the trunk and the opposite side of the ravine.

I decided to go for it.

I jerked the bike's handlebars toward the ravine and bunny-hopped off the trail, down onto the tree trunk. My landing was solid, but my feet slipped off the stupid pedal clips that weren't connected to my shoes. The bike began to wobble and buck, and I had no choice but to ditch it. I couldn't fall to either side, so I threw myself over the handlebars.

I sprawled in midair, landing on the tree trunk with one arm and one leg dangling over each side. I probably don't need to tell you that it hurt. A lot. I looked down and watched as DaXing's mountain bike tumbled end over end on its way to the ravine floor. It landed with a metallic thunk atop a rock-strewn streambed.

I felt the trunk begin to sway, and I glanced back to see that DaXing was climbing down onto it!

I scrambled to my feet. The rubber and metal bottoms of my shoes got surprisingly good traction on the trunk's rough bark. Perhaps I could get some speed and make the jump from the end of the trunk to the opposite side of the ravine? I began to weigh my odds of success when I heard the tree trunk's roots begin to pop.

I turned to see that DaXing had made his way fully onto the trunk. As he advanced toward me, the popping intensified, and the entire tree began to tilt from an upward angle to a downward one.

It was now or never.

I sprinted to the end of the trunk and leaped as high and as far as I could. I imagined I was riding a BMX bike, soaring dozens of feet into the air off of one of Raffi's perfect dirt jumps.

It worked.

I landed pretty hard, but I was a full five feet away from the ravine's edge.

Things didn't go as well for DaXing. I watched as the tree roots completely gave way, and he and the tree trunk went speeding to the bottom of the ravine. DaXing hit the rocky streamed first, followed by the trunk directly on top of his chest, shoulders, and head. He was still wearing his biking helmet, but of course it didn't matter. An army helmet wouldn't even have helped. He was now just as broken as his bicycle, which lay near him.

I turned away from the terrible sight and vomited huevos rancheros until my throat ached. Once the retching stopped, I rinsed my mouth with water from the hydration pack and wiped tears from my eyes. Some of the tears were for me, but most were for DaXing. I hated that that had to happen to him.

I pulled my cell phone out of my mud-soaked riding shorts and stared at it. It was dirty and wet, but encased in a watertight enclosure. It would work just fine.

But whom should I call?

Calling 911 would be the right thing to do, but it wasn't like anybody would be able to do anything for DaXing. As for his remains, the police would want to know what happened to him, but at what cost to me? My parents would find out what I was up to, and I would be dragged into an investigation. An investigation would delay my trip to China. Worse than that, my parents would *cancel* my trip, for sure, for having rented the limo and come out here in the first place. Then I would have Hú Dié's mother's death on my hands as well as DaXing's.

That would be too much to bear. I needed to get the heck out of the park and fly to China as soon as possible. Once I'd delivered the dragon bone to Hú Dié, I'd decide what to do about DaXing, if anything.

I stood and tried to get my bearings. The bike trail was a loop, and I was certain that it went all the way around this ravine. All I had to do was find the trail on this side and follow it around to the silty hill, where I could retrieve my bike. Then I could ride back to the limo with the dragon bone and hightail it home. It was 3:30 p.m., so I was still good on time.

I started walking, keeping my eyes peeled for the bike trail.

It was 4:30 p.m. by the time I found my mountain bike beneath the pine tree in the fern grove. It was getting down to the wire time-wise, but instead of grabbing my bike and hitting the trail, I headed for the mushroom patch. I needed to find the rake.

I realized that there was a good chance it could be traced back to me or my parents. I was wearing full-fingered riding gloves at the moment, but the rake likely had my fingerprints on it from handling it earlier. It probably had my mother and father's fingerprints on it, too; it definitely had DaXing's fingerprints from when he threw it at me. The rake could also have some of his blood on it, as well as skin or other tissue on the tines.

I needed to get it back.

I recalled the rake hitting my helmet after DaXing and I rolled out of the stinkhorn patch, and I had to think for a minute before I found it. The rake did indeed have some blood on the handle, as well as creepy bits dangling from the ends of the tines. I gave it a quick wipe-down with some leaves, then hit the trail.

Hard.

I raced back to the parking lot with the rake in one hand. It was nearly five p.m. when I pulled up beside the limo and knocked on the half-open driver's-side window to wake up Michael. He took one look at me with the rake and nearly jumped out of his seat.

He lowered the window. "What the heck are you trying to do, give me a heart attack? I thought you were the Grim Reaper!"

"The Grim Reaper carries a scythe," I said. "Not a mini rake."

"Whatever," he said. "It still ain't right. Have you seen yourself? You're a mess."

I glanced down at my arms, legs, and torso. He was right, I *was* a mess.

Michael sniffed the air through his open window and made a funny face. "What's that awful smell?"

"I accidentally fell into a patch of stinkhorn mushrooms."

"What the heck were you and your girlfriend doing out there? You're dirtier than your bike."

"Clawing at stream banks," I lied. "We were looking for old Native American arrowheads. We just used our bikes to get to the spot faster. She rode in from a different trail."

That seemed to satisfy him. "Oh," he said. "That's pretty cool. Did you have any luck?"

"I found one thing, but I'm going to let her keep it."

"What a gentleman. I hope it was worth all the trouble."

"Trouble?" I asked, looking around. There was no one else in the parking lot.

"I don't mean trouble with somebody else, I mean trouble with *me*. I can't let you get into the limo like that."

"But how am I supposed to get home?"

"I don't know. Call your folks, maybe?"

I frowned. "Don't you have a tarp or blankets or something in the trunk?"

"This isn't an emergency tow truck," Michael said. "I don't have anything like that. You don't happen to have a change of clothes inside that grubby backpack, do you?"

I shook my head, and my mind began to race. "Hey," I said. "Maybe you could buy me some?"

"I'm a chauffeur, not a personal shopper. Besides, the nearest store is miles from here. We're in the middle of nowhere."

"They have a lodge. Check the map the ranger gave you at the gate. There's even a water park with a gift shop where they sell towels and t-shirts and stuff. I think they have bathing suits. I could wear one of those and a t-shirt."

Michael groaned, reaching for the map. "This is going to cost you."

"I have cash." I pulled my wallet out from my riding shorts. It was covered with filth, but I was certain that everything inside was fine. The wallet was rubber, made from old bike inner tubes, and the top zipped shut. I'd ridden in a bunch of rainstorms without my money getting even a little damp.

Michael's face twisted with disgust. "How about you wash that thing off first? I'll pay for your new clothes. You'll pay me back *triple* when I return. Deal?"

"Deal."

"I'll be right back," Michael said. "See if you can find a creek or something. You're going to have to rinse off those clothes, too, before I can throw them into the trunk."

I pointed to a building across the road. "That's a restroom. It has running water. Meet me over there."

Michael nodded and pulled away.

I put my wallet back into the pocket of my soggy riding shorts and sighed. I really was a mess. This whole situation was one gigantic, expensive, deadly mess.

I rode across the street and waited for Michael to return.

Michael arrived at the restroom much faster than I'd expected. He'd had extremely good luck. He not only found me a t-shirt, board shorts, and two beach towels, but he'd also picked up a pair of flip-flops that fit perfectly. When I stepped out of the restroom, I was a completely different kid.

"Whoa, I hardly recognize you," Michael said. "If it wasn't for all that shaggy hair, you'd almost look human."

"Gee, thanks," I said. "Let's get out of here. I kind of plugged up all three sinks."

Michael laughed, and I handed him the plastic shopping bag that now contained my rinsed-off clothes and riding shoes. He put the bag into the trunk and hung my bike on the bike rack, and we hit the road.

It felt great to be back inside the limo again. The ride was smooth, and the air-conditioning was soothing. I'd cleaned up the hydration backpack to Michael's standards, and it was on the floor beside me. The pack was weather-resistant, and it had done a perfect job of keeping the silk bag of dragon bone clean and dry. I wanted to call Hú Dié and let her know about my success, but she was on a plane by now. I wouldn't get a chance to talk with her for at least a full day, maybe two. She was flying first to Chicago, then to Beijing, then on to Kaifeng and straight to see her mother. The only phone number I had for her was her home/bike shop number, but she said that she was going to try to pick up an international cell phone. She would probably call me before I would be able to catch her at home.

While I couldn't call Hú Dié, I could call Ryan. He was bound to be awake by now. I'd put my cell phone and wallet into the backpack with the bag of dragon bone a while ago, so I pulled my phone back out. I was surprised to see that Ryan and Phoenix had been blowing it up with voicemails. There was also a voicemail from my dad. I checked the ringer and saw that it was turned off. I turned it back on and was about to start listening to the messages when the phone rang.

It was Ryan's home number. I answered it.

"Ryan?" I said. "What's up?"

"Haven't you listened to my voicemails?" he asked. "Or Phoenix's? He's been trying to reach you, too."

"I haven't listened to anything yet. I was away from my phone."

"We have a problem," Ryan said.

I felt a knot forming in the pit of my stomach. "What kind of problem?"

"Phoenix and I can't go to China. At least, not right now."

That wasn't at all what I was expecting to hear.

"Why not?" I asked.

"Because of everything that happened in California and Texas," Ryan said. "The police in both states want us to stick around in case they need us for anything."

"Stick around? How long?"

"They said that it shouldn't be more than a couple days, so maybe we'll still be able to ride in the big race. You've been cleared, though."

"I have?"

"Yes. My mom already asked. The police said that you were just a very small part of the California investigation, and they already have everything they'll need from you. You weren't in Texas with me, Phoenix, and Hú Dié, so no worries there."

My heart skipped a beat. "Hú Dié? Are they making her stay, too?"

"The police wanted her to stay, but Ling and Mr. Chang got involved. Those guys can pull some serious strings. Her plane already took off."

"Whew," I said. "That's good. She really needs to be with her mother. Is there anything else going on?"

"In case you didn't know, your parents have already talked with Ling and Mr. Chang."

"*My* parents?"

"Yeah. My mom called your mom earlier, and your mom called Ling. Your dad has talked with him, too. Your parents seem pretty excited about you riding in China. I think they've already made your travel arrangements."

"My dad left me a voicemail message, but I haven't listened to it, either. He was in court all day. I guess he's out."

"Duh," Ryan said. "It's like six forty-five."

I checked the time on my phone, and I felt my eyes bulge out of my head. It really *was* 6:45 p.m.! I wouldn't arrive until almost eight p.m. My dad might get home before me.

"I gotta go," I said. "I need to listen to my dad's message. Should I call Phoenix?"

"If you want to. He'll probably just tell you the same stuff I just told you, though."

"Right," I said. "I'll catch up with him some other time. I really need to listen to my dad's message."

"Roger that," Ryan said. "Keep me posted."

"Ten-four," I said. "Over and out."

I ended the call.

Wow. Things were getting more insane by the minute. I felt bad that Ryan and Phoenix were going to have to wait before being allowed to travel to China, but part of me was relieved. It would make life a lot easier for me if they weren't around at first, especially Phoenix.

I scrolled through my voicemail messages and found my dad's:

Jake, you must be asleep. Good for you. Guess the jet lag set in. Just want to let you know that your mother and I have both been in touch with Ling and Mr. Chang. You've probably heard about Ryan and Phoenix by now and their situation, but you are good to go. In fact, you're booked on a flight to China tomorrow evening. Your mother and I have both taken tomorrow off of work so that we can spend a little family time together and take you to the airport. I'm going to have to work extra late tonight to make up for missing court tomorrow, but I think it's worth it. I should see you around nine p.m. If you wake up before I get home, order a big greasy pizza for delivery and relax. You're going to need all the rest you can get. It sounds like Ling and Mr. Chang have big plans for you! Congratulations, son! We're so proud of you! See you soon!

The message ended.

I sighed with relief. I would make it home well before he did. It would be fun hanging out with them tomorrow, too.

I realized that I was getting hungry, but the thought of greasy pizza turned my stomach. I'd probably just make a sandwich or something when I got home. I'd thrown away all the energy bars I'd brought with me in the pocket of my riding shorts because they'd been doused with stinkhorn mud.

I listened to my voicemails from Phoenix and Ryan, and found that they echoed one another. I considered calling Ryan again to let him know about my flight plans, but I decided to wait until tomorrow for that, too. I didn't want to bum him out any more today. He'd had enough bad news. He wanted to travel and race a lot more than I did, but he was going to be stuck at home while I flew halfway around the world to ride.

I tried to think if there was anyone else I needed to call, or anything else I needed to do. Only one thing came to mind. I leaned forward and knocked on the glass separating Michael and me.

He lowered the long window.

"What's up?" he asked.

I pulled my wallet out of my backpack. "Can we settle up right now? I'd feel weird handing you a bunch of cash in a grocery store parking lot."

"Good idea."

"What do I owe you?"

"Besides the three hundred dollars for the limo? Let's see, I spent fifty dollars at the gift shop, so triple that is a hundred-fifty dollars. Plus a tip."

"How much do people usually tip?"

"Depends how happy they are with my service. Most people give me twenty percent, because I'm awesome."

I rolled my eyes and did some quick math. Twenty percent of $300 was $60. And $360 plus $150 equaled $510.

I unzipped my wallet and looked inside. I'd brought every dime I had, which equaled $540. I gave it all to him. I was *very* happy with his service. I also hoped a big tip would help him keep his mouth shut. He didn't have any clue what had happened out on the bike trail, and the fewer people who knew I was even at the state park, the better. Someone was bound to find DaXing eventually.

"Hey, thanks!" Michael said. "You can call me anytime!"

"I'll remember that," I said. "How much longer before we get back?"

"Half an hour. Maybe forty-five minutes. Sit back and enjoy the ride."

I nodded, and Michael raised the window back up.

I thought again about what else I had to do. It was clear that all the wheels had been set in motion. There was literally nothing else I could do, except take Michael's advice and sit back and enjoy the ride.

So I did.

STAGE THREE

It never gets easier; you just go faster.
—Greg LeMond,
American cycling legend

My plane left for Shanghai as scheduled the next day. I'd had a nice time with my parents beforehand, as well as brief conversations with Ryan and Phoenix. Phoenix still had no clue what I'd done. I felt kind of bad about it, but not bad enough to say anything. Somebody had to help Hú Dié, and he wasn't doing squat.

Hú Dié made it to Kaifeng, and she sent me an email. She'd bought a new cell phone, but it would only work in China. She gave me the number anyway, and I memorized it. I emailed back that I was on my way to Shanghai, and she replied that she already knew. Ling had told her. She wasn't sure when she'd be able to make it down to Shanghai, though, because her mother was really bad, so I offered to try to come to Kaifeng. I said that she'd be "very happy to see me." She replied with a smiley face. I wasn't sure if Ling would actually allow me go to Kaifeng, but I didn't care. I would figure out a way if I had to. Racing was important to me, but my friends were more important. I couldn't let Hú Dié down.

The plane landed after an incredibly boring fifteen-hour nonstop flight, and I piled out of the cabin with the other passengers. I'd never been so happy to see the inside of an airport in my life. We were led along a corridor that exited into a huge space with lines of travelers queued up to pass through one of more than a dozen immigration lanes.

I took a deep breath and adjusted my carry-on backpack over my shoulder. I had the dragon bone inside a container of protein powder. The security officers at Indianapolis International Airport didn't seem to think anything of it, especially since I had special travel documents that said I was going to China to race bicycles. I hoped the immigration and customs officials here would feel the same way. If they figured out I had dragon bone, there was no telling what might happen to me.

Someone called out my name.

"Jake! Over here!"

It was Ling. He waved to me from the farthest lane, which was fancier than the others and completely empty. Next to Ling was a decorative sign printed in English and Chinese. The English read DIPLOMATS ONLY.

"This way!" Ling shouted to me. "No need for *you* to wait in a line!"

How embarrassing. I hoped this wasn't the way I was going to be treated the entire time I was in China.

I wove my way through the crowd, over to Ling, and shook his hand.

"So good to see you!" Ling said cheerily.

"Same," I replied. And I meant it. It was a little scary arriving alone in a foreign country.

I handed my passport and travel papers to the immigration officer, and she stamped my passport with an entry visa after checking to make sure that my face matched my passport photo. Ling then led me over to another special line, this one for customs. He flashed some type of ID card, and we were waved through without any sort of inspection.

I sighed with relief. Nobody was going to look inside my backpack.

We exited through a set of huge glass doors, into the main airport terminal. Hundreds of happy Chinese people were behind a long line of velvet ropes, ready to greet arriving friends and family members. Many of the people waiting held colorful gift bags and huge bouquets of flowers. It was really cool. The whole place buzzed with excitement.

I grinned.

Ling smiled back. "Welcome to Shanghai. I think you're going to like it here. We are very warm people."

"It sure seems that way," I said.

I followed Ling outside to a waiting minivan, where there was a young guy seated behind the wheel. The weather was warm, just like Indiana, and it was getting dark out, which was very odd because it had been getting dark when I'd boarded the plane. Shanghai time was twelve hours ahead of Indiana time, plus I'd been in the air fifteen hours. I'd lost twenty-seven hours of my life on that flight. I was trying to get my head around this when I suddenly realized that we'd forgotten something—my luggage.

"Wait!" I said. "We need to go to baggage claim. I checked a suitcase."

Ling shook his head. "Already taken care of." He pointed to the back of the minivan.

I peered through the window. Sure enough, there was my suitcase.

The minivan's driver got out and opened the large rear door, and Ling reached for my backpack.

I reflexively jerked away.

Ling frowned at me. "I was just going to put your pack alongside your suitcase for you. Why the extreme reaction? Are you hiding something from me?"

"No," I lied. "My, um, wallet and passport are in there. So is my tablet. I guess I'm just a little jumpy about it. Phoenix once told me how somebody tried to steal his backpack when he was in China."

Ling raised an eyebrow. "Is that all? Okay, then."

I handed over my backpack, and Ling put it into the back of the minivan without looking inside it. The driver closed the back door. I climbed into one of the backseats as Ling and the driver got into the front seats. They exchanged a few words in Chinese, and the driver pulled out into the approaching night.

We were soon on a major highway that looked a lot like the multi-lane highway leading away from Indianapolis International Airport. If I hadn't just seen and heard all the Chinese people in the terminal, I would have guessed we were back in the States.

Ling turned around and handed me a cell phone. "You should call your parents and let them know that you've arrived safely. Your mother's number is already on the screen. Just hit *send*."

I hit *send*. My mom picked up a few seconds later.

"Hello?" she said. "Ling?"

"No, Mom," I said. "It's me, Jake."

"Baby! You made it?"

"Yep."

"How are you?"

"Great."

"No problems?"

"Nope. It's kind of weird that it's getting dark here, but I know it's just a time zone thing."

"You'll adjust to it," my mom said. "Do you need anything?"

"No. Ling is taking care of me. I didn't have to wait in a single line at the airport. He's the man."

"I'm so glad that you're in good hands. Enjoy yourself, baby."

"For sure," I said. "I'd better go, so I can give Ling back his cell phone."

"Okay," my mother said. "Goodbye for now. I'll let your father know that you're well!"

"Thanks. I'll call you in a couple days."

"You do that. We'll call Ling if we need to reach you in the meantime. Have fun!"

My mom hung up, and I handed the phone back to Ling. "Thanks," I said.

"Don't mention it," Ling replied. "So, how much do you know about Shanghai?"

"Not a lot."

"You didn't research the city to which you were traveling?"

"No, but my mom sort of did. She told me that it's big."

"It's the most populated city in the world. More than twenty-three million people live here."

"No way," I said. "That's *huge.*"

"It is. It doesn't always feel big, though. There are two main halves, Puxi and Pudong, which are separated by the Huangpu River."

"Isn't one old and one new?" I asked.

"Yes. Puxi is to the west, and it's the historic trading and banking center of Shanghai. The east side of the river is Pudong, which is kind of like 'new' Shanghai. That is where all the famous skyscrapers are and such. It is also where most of the growth and expansion is happening. You will be staying on the outskirts of Pudong in a very new, very Western area. You won't find it much different from the United States, as I believe I've already told you."

I stared out the window at all the streetlights and illuminated buildings. "I already don't find it much different from the United States. If it wasn't for the signs being in Chinese, I'd swear I was back in Indianapolis or even Los Angeles. I can see the haze of smog in the lights. Or is it fog? We're by the ocean, right?"

"We are very near the ocean, yes. Shanghai is the largest port in the world. However, what you are seeing is smog, not fog. It is a bit of an embarrassment, but it is the price we pay for having so many people and so much industry. We are doing our best to manage the situation, including daily

pollution-count announcements. You will get used to checking them each morning. If the levels are too high, you will
train inside rather than outside."

"It's *that* bad?"

"It can be. Most buildings have air-filtration systems,
though. We simply stay inside on bad days."

I shook my head, unable to comprehend not being able
to go outside. I continued to stare out the window, watching
as we turned off the highway onto a crowded street with
two lanes of traffic going in each direction. Along either
side of the street was a wide bike lane separated from the
traffic by a waist-high wall; next to each bike lane was a
sidewalk. There were hundreds of bicyclists using the lane,
along with hundreds more on motor scooters and mopeds.
The sidewalks were packed with people walking. Most of
the pedestrians and nearly every single rider either wore a
surgical mask or had some type of scarf wrapped over his or
her nose and mouth.

"As you can see," Ling said, "today there is a high pollution count. Hence, all the covered faces. While people
remain inside as much as possible on a day like today, they
still have to travel to and from work."

I nodded, trying not to think about the pollution.
Instead, I focused on the bikes. I saw more different styles
in two minutes than I'd seen in my entire life in the States.
We passed bicycle taxis, bicycle vending carts, and bicycles
with trailers containing construction supplies. We even
passed a guy riding some sort of oversized delivery bike that
had so many plastic milk jugs strapped to the back, they
reached the height of a second-story window.

Ling must have read my mind. "So many different uses for bicycles, no?"

"Yeah. I had no idea. I think I get what you and Mr. Chang are trying to do. People here think of bikes as a way to get around, not as a sport."

"Exactly. I thought it would make more sense to you once you arrived."

The minivan slowed for a traffic light, and I saw a huge line of people in front of a small shop. Ling powered down his window, and the oily smell of fried food wafted into the minivan. It wasn't very appetizing.

"Are you hungry?" he asked. "Shanghai is famous for its dumplings, and this place is one of the best."

"No thanks," I said. "I ate on the plane."

"Have you ever tried traditional Shanghai dumplings?"

"No."

"Well, do yourself a favor and try some while you are here. I've never met anyone who didn't like *xiao long bao*. People eat them at any hour, even for breakfast."

"Okay," I said.

We continued on through the night, merging onto another highway. I couldn't help noticing a long row of illuminated billboards that looked like the ones you'd see in America, except these all had Chinese writing on them. It was surreal, because several of the billboards featured American actors selling different products. Then there was a billboard for—

"What the—" I began, but couldn't find the words to continue.

Ling laughed. "Impressive, isn't it?"

One of the billboards was a picture of *me,* along with Phoenix, Ryan, and Hú Dié road bike racing in California. It also showed four Chinese guys who were about the same age as us. They were dressed in matching road cycling uniforms and posed as a team. One of the riders was standing in front of the others as if he were the leader. He was really skinny and had messy black hair as well as close-set, beady eyes. He looked like a psychopath. I had no idea what the billboard said because, of course, the text was in Chinese.

"You and your friends are *big* in China," Ling said, still laughing. "Literally! What do you think?"

"It's the craziest thing I've ever seen!" I said, pulling my cell phone from my pocket. The phone didn't work in China, but the camera would. I snapped off a couple shots before we passed the billboard.

"Seriously," I said. "That's nuts."

"No, that's the publicity machine in motion. Several of those billboards have gone up on both sides of the river. By race time, half of Shanghai will recognize your face."

I put my phone away. "Who is the other team?"

"Yes, the other team," Ling said. "I suppose we should discuss that. When you told us that you needed time to consider our offer, Mr. Chang realized that he needed a backup plan. Specifically, he needed a backup *team.* He made some phone calls, and our trainers put together a group of talented young Chinese riders. They wouldn't settle for playing the role of backup, though, and Mr. Chang decided that there really was no reason for that. They should be allowed to compete alongside you and your friends as well as the entire field of adult participants. May the best team win, if you will. If the young Chinese team wins, well . . . then you and your friends will go home and they will be the official poster team. If *you* win, then you will have the opportunity to stay, if you'd like, and be the poster team."

I felt my jaws clench. "That wasn't the deal."

"Your indecision forced this upon us, Jake. Moreover, it is uncertain whether US officials will even allow Phoenix and Ryan to travel here in time to participate in the race. We needed a contingency plan, and now we have one."

"So what happens to me if Phoenix and Ryan can't make it? I'm out?"

"No. Mr. Chang has decided that you and Hú Dié will still race as a team."

"Just the two of us?"

"Yes."

"We'll get killed!" I said, nearly jumping out of my seat. "Two against four isn't a fair fight in a road bike race. They'll have twice as many people to rotate through their lead rider position. The lead rider pulls the *entire team* along in the slipstream."

Ling shrugged. "It isn't our fault that two of your riders may not be able to attend the race. Perhaps you now see the wisdom of Mr. Chang's decision to assemble a second team of youths."

I rolled my eyes, but Ling was right. From their perspective, it *was* a good plan. From mine, however, it meant that my trip here was pointless as far as the race was concerned if Phoenix and Ryan wouldn't be here in time. Hú Dié might as well not even bother to show up if it was just going to be the two of us. I had to contact her as soon as possible. Maybe we could figure out a way for me to go to Kaifeng, drop off the dragon bone, and then head straight home. There was no point in just her and me racing. We'd make fools of ourselves in front of twenty-three million people.

I sat back and turned away from Ling. I doubted this trip could get much worse.

14

We arrived at the apartment complex, and it was just like Ling said it would be. It was very new and very large, and the neighborhood looked just like America. Even the street and building signs were in English.

I grabbed my backpack, and Ling grabbed my suitcase. Ling said a few words in Chinese to the driver, and the driver left.

"Keep an eye out for that same minivan tomorrow morning at seven a.m. sharp," Ling told me. "There may be a different driver, but the vehicle will not change. You will return here around eight p.m. That will be your daily schedule right up to the race, seven a.m. to eight p.m."

"That's a long day," I said.

"You have much work to do. Being a celebrity is a round-the-clock job."

I sighed and followed Ling up a set of concrete stairs into the apartment complex. We passed through a set of gates, and I saw that the complex was even bigger than I'd imagined from the street. At least twenty ten-story buildings surrounded a huge courtyard.

"How many apartments are in here?" I asked.

"Several thousand. It's the largest concentration of Westerners in China. You'll feel right at home."

We entered one of the ten-story buildings, and Ling nodded to a security guard stationed beside the front door. The security guard nodded back.

"Jake, this is Loo," Ling said. "Loo, meet Jake."

Loo grinned. "Hello, Jake," he said in perfect English. "Pleased to meet you. I saw your picture next to the highway."

"Nice to meet you, too, Loo. That picture is kind of embarrassing."

"No, it's not," Loo said. "Maybe if your legs were shaved like most adult cyclists', then it would be embarrassing."

I laughed. "Good point."

Ling turned to me. "If you have any questions about the neighborhood or need anything, Loo is your man."

"Got it," I said.

"This is building number three. Your apartment is number one. Just remember three-oh-one."

"Check," I said. "Three-oh-one."

We climbed up an interior staircase to a long hallway that had several different apartment doors. Mine was the first one. Ling inserted a key into the lock, and we went in.

The apartment was pretty sweet. It had new furniture and was bigger than most people's houses. In fact, it looked like you could fit at least two of Phoenix's house inside here.

"There are three large bedrooms and three bathrooms,"

Ling said. "You will share this apartment with Phoenix and Ryan, if they make it. Hú Dié will stay in apartment three-oh-two across the hall. It's smaller than this one, but not by much. Residents here receive visits every other day from an *ayee*, or housekeeper. Many of the *ayees* also cook and will buy your groceries, too, if you give them money in advance. Your *ayee* is a wonderful chef, and we've made arrangements for her to have plenty of money to keep you well fed."

"Wow. Thanks."

He handed me his key and said, "I have copies of this key back at my office, so no funny business. I will be making periodic checks on you. I am also arranging to get a cell phone for you to stay connected with me at all times. I should have it by tomorrow. Do you have any questions?"

"Um, I don't think so. This is all coming at me kind of fast."

Ling placed a hand on my shoulder. "It is, Jake, but you'll be fine. I realize that you've probably never been in a situation like this before. Your parents told me that when you trained in California, you lived with your coach as well as your friends. Would you like me to make arrangements to have an adult stay with you?"

"No, I'm good. I'll be even better after a nap. I didn't sleep a whole lot on the plane."

"I'll leave you, then. There is just one more thing before I go. Follow me out to the balcony."

I tossed my backpack onto the living room couch and stepped outside with Ling through a sliding glass door. The night air was still warm and humid. I couldn't see a single star, but the lights from restaurants and shops shone just a few hundred yards away across a park.

"Well?" Ling asked. "What do you think?"

"It's a great view," I said.

Ling chuckled. "You *must* be tired, Jake. I wasn't referring to the view." He pointed to the opposite end of the balcony. "Look."

I turned around and saw a brand-new BMX bike. It looked to be the perfect size for me, and was tricked out with more bling than a jewelry store. A skater-style helmet hung from the handlebars—exactly the type freestyle BMX riders wore.

"For me?" I asked.

Ling nodded. "A little token of our appreciation for you coming here. It's yours to take back to the States, if you'd like. We realize that road bike racing isn't your passion. Saturday's race is simply a means of gaining you notoriety. If you stay, you will choose which type or types of cycling you want to promote."

I couldn't help grinning. "Thanks a ton! I wasn't expecting this."

"I'm glad to see you smiling," Ling said. "Let me leave on that note. There is an alarm clock in each bedroom. Make sure you set one and leave yourself plenty of time to get ready in the morning. As I said, you will be picked up downstairs at seven a.m. sharp. You will be driven to our makeshift training facility about half an hour away. Mr. Chang is looking for a permanent location for a mega-training center, but that will take a couple more weeks of scouting. The good news is, things happen very fast in China. Once a location is found, we'll be up and running in just a few months. You're here at a very exciting time, Jake."

"No doubt," I said. "Are you going to be there tomorrow?"

"Of course. I will be there every day, and—"

I heard a snicker, and a voice said, *"This is my competition? Ha!"*

I whipped around and saw someone standing on the neighboring balcony. The person flipped on an outside light, and I realized that it was the lead kid of the Chinese team that Mr. Chang had put together to challenge us. The kid looked even skinnier and more psychotic in real life.

"Good evening, Keng," Ling said. "This is Jake."

"I know who it is," Keng replied, and he spat over the balcony to the sidewalk below.

"Nice to meet you," I said.

"Yep," Keng replied. "It *is* nice for you to meet me. Too bad I don't feel the same way about meeting you. Why don't you go back where you came from?"

I felt my eyes narrow. "I—"

"That is enough, Keng," Ling interrupted. "Don't take the bait, Jake. Keng is just trying to rile you up."

"I know that, and he's doing a pretty good job," I said, "but I don't mind a little trash talk. It just motivates me more. Make sure you put on your big-boy shoes on Saturday, Keng. I'm going to show you how us Americans roll."

Keng scowled and said something in Chinese.

Ling shook his head and ushered me inside.

"What did he say?" I asked.

"Something about you almost losing to a girl in California. It's not important."

"What a gasbag," I said. "I'd like to see how *he* does against Hú Dié. She's awesome. You guys recruited him as a possible poster boy?"

"He's an amazing rider. Mr. Chang believes that Keng can be taught to behave better if he and his team win on Saturday. Personally, I'm rooting for your team, Jake. I would rather not work with Keng for years. Please don't tell anyone I said that, though."

"My lips are sealed. Thanks, Ling."

"My pleasure," he replied, and he reached into one of his pockets. He pulled out a wad of Chinese bills and handed some to me. "Here's some pocket money," he said. "Buy whatever you'd like. There are plenty of souvenir shops in this neighborhood, as well as a wealth of stores that carry snacks and the like."

"Are you sure? My folks exchanged a bunch of money for me at the airport back in Indiana."

"I'm positive," Ling said. "Take your new bike for a spin around the neighborhood sometime. Treat yourself."

"I will," I said. "See you, and thanks again."

Ling nodded and left, and I locked the door behind him. The last thing I needed was Keng to come barging in here. He seemed exactly like the kind of kid who'd do that.

I actually was getting a little hungry, so I hit the kitchen. The cupboards were indeed full, but most of what I saw was protein powders and vitamins. I wondered how much of this stuff they actually wanted me to take. The less, the better, as far as I was concerned.

There were a few different kinds of fruit in the refrigerator, but nothing really jumped out at me. The freezer was packed, too, but only with various types of frozen Chinese dumplings. What was up with people from Shanghai and dumplings?

I gave up on the food and checked out the rest of the apartment. All of the bedrooms were the same size, shape, and color, and they all had identical bathrooms. I went back to the living room, where Ling had left my suitcase, and took it to the bedroom farthest from the living room. I figured it would be the quietest. I was going to unpack, but I didn't feel like it. I was tired, but I didn't really feel like sleeping.

I checked the clock and saw that it was nearly eight p.m. The sun set early here this time of year. If I went to sleep now, I might wake up in the middle of the night and be unable to fall back asleep. Jet lag did things like that to people. It would be better for me to stay up a couple more hours before crashing for the night at my normal Indiana time like my mom had suggested. Phoenix once told me that Chinese people tended to stay up late, and therefore shops usually stayed open late. Based on all the lights I'd seen from the balcony, that seemed to be the case. Maybe I'd take my new bike for a little spin and find something to eat.

I went out to the balcony and found that, thankfully, Keng was no longer there. I strapped on the helmet and threw the BMX bike over my shoulder, then grabbed my backpack and left. I carried the bike down the interior stairs, nodding to Loo, the security guard.

"Heading out for a ride?" Loo asked. "Searching for anything in particular? Dumplings, perhaps?"

I rolled my eyes. "Not dumplings, but I am kind of hungry. I think I'm just going to wing it, though."

"Go anywhere you'd like, except I strongly suggest that you not cross under the highway into Old Town."

"Why not? Foreigners aren't welcome there?"

"It's not so much that. The streets are covered in rubble. No one bothers to ride bicycles there because they experience far too many tire punctures. Also, no one speaks English. A few of the Americans who live here venture into Old Town about once a month to grab a bite to eat, but that's only because the dumpling shops there are the very best in the entire city."

"Sounds like I won't be missing much."

"Exactly," Loo said. "Be safe."

"I will. See you in an hour or so."

"I'll be here."

Loo held the door for me, and I pushed my new BMX bike outside, into the warm night. I was wearing the same t-shirt and cargo shorts that I'd worn on the plane, and they were beginning to feel a little sticky. It didn't matter, though, as I was bound to work up a sweat cruising around here. I'd just shower once I returned.

I walked my bike through the main gates and then jumped on, riding down the concrete stairs. The bike handled them like a dream. It had been far too long since I'd bombed down steps. I hit the sidewalk and began to pedal, searching for more stairs or other things to ride.

I'd forgotten how much fun this was, just cruising around. Out here, I was part of the street, not riding someone else's trails. Street riding was all about breaking the rules and riding something that wasn't meant to be ridden. I kept my eyes peeled for setups—ledges, wedges, rails, ramps, whatever.

I soon found a low rail and bunny-hopped onto it, doing a perfect pedal grind that lasted almost five seconds. It was awesome. Next, I came across a small loading dock at the back of a clothing shop. The dock had a ramp that looked pretty sketchy, but I hit it anyway. I caught some sweet air and landed with a fluidity that reminded me why I loved BMX so much. It was all about flow and creating new lines.

BMX was whatever you wanted it to be.

I circled around to the front of the clothing shop and saw a line of people waiting to get into a movie theater next door. Two girls about my age pointed at me and began to giggle excitedly. I was pretty sure they'd seen my face on the billboard. I had to admit, it felt pretty good. I decided to give them a little show. There was a low bench nearby that didn't have anyone sitting on it, so I bunny-hopped over the whole thing.

The girls squealed with delight and clapped their hands. "More! More!" they shouted in English.

Who was I to let them down? I leaned back into a man-ual, which was basically a wheelie without pedaling, and cruised the length of the line. More people began to clap.

This really *was* fun. There was an old guy riding past on an ancient delivery bike, and even he stopped to watch from the bike lane next to the road. I nodded to him and pulled off a series of flatland moves that I hadn't attempted in years. Flatland was essentially doing every kind of trick imaginable on your bike without actually riding or falling off of it. I climbed up and down the handlebars, balanced on the front and back tires, and stood one-legged on the bike frame's downtube, all without losing my balance a single time. The people waiting in line seemed impressed, as did the old guy. He clapped wildly and flashed me a huge, toothless grin.

I stepped off my bike to consider my next series of moves when I noticed a cyclist cruising toward me. He rode a high-end road bike and was decked out in a complete European road bike racing kit, complete with full-fingered gloves. He was wearing a helmet and nighttime riding glasses, plus a silk scarf that covered most of his face. I realized that he was wrapped head to toe, as if it were the middle of winter. But it was summer.

He spoke, and his words hit me like a punch to the stomach.

"Hello, Jake."

I recognized that voice.

It was Lin Tan.

15

I locked eyes with Lin Tan in front of the long line of movie-goers. This was the guy who was supposed to have washed out to sea after having been poisoned to death by DuSow's deadly touch. I instinctively tightened the straps on my backpack because this was bound to get ugly, and there was no way that I was going to get separated from the dragon bone.

"You're alive," I said.

"Clearly," Lin Tan said, "a little worse for wear but, yes, still alive. Imagine my surprise when I stepped off of a smuggler's airplane here in Shanghai to see your face on a billboard. Who would have guessed? I've spent my entire career attempting to popularize cycling in my native country, and what happens? My country imports a blond, shaggy-haired foreigner to do it instead."

"There's no guarantee that I'll be the one they pick," I

said. "You'd have just as good a chance. Are you planning to race on Saturday?"

"Ha! My racing days are over, as are my days of posing for magazine ads like I used to. Billboards like yours are definitely out of the question." He pulled off his riding glasses and scarf, and nearly everyone in the movie line shrieked. Several of them even ran off.

I swallowed a lump of bile that had risen into my throat. Lin Tan's skin was coal black and scaly, like that of a melanistic lizard. His eyes had sunken deep into their sockets, and his eyebrows had fallen off.

"This is the end result of DuSow's poison," Lin Tan said. "I suppose I should be grateful that the dragon bone I'd once taken or its poison-based antidote somehow protected me from death, but it's difficult to feel grateful for anything when you look like this. You have no idea what lengths I had to go to to find passage back to China. And when I arrive, what do I find? Like I said, *you!*"

"Why do you have a problem with me?" I asked. "I've never done anything to you."

"You played a role in the sequence of events that led to DuSow taking action against me. For that, you will pay."

"But—"

Lin Tan dropped his bike and lunged at me. I stepped back, holding my bike in front of me like a shield, but he grabbed it. He tore it from my grasp and hurled it to one side. I turned to run, but he took hold of my backpack. I pulled with all my might, and he held fast.

The pack couldn't take the strain.

I heard fabric tear, and there was a soft crack as the plastic protein powder container hit the sidewalk. I spun around and snatched up the container, cupping one hand over the small opening that had formed along the bottom seam.

Lin Tan saw the protein powder label and froze. He picked up a pinch of gray powder that had poured out onto the concrete, and he sniffed it. His spooky eyes went wide.

"Dragon bone!" he said.

I jumped on my bike with the container tucked under one arm. I held it upside down so that no more would spill out.

I began to pedal away, and Lin Tan screamed, "Get back here!"

As if.

I hammered as hard as I could for about ten seconds, then I risked a glance over my shoulder. Lin Tan was standing still while reaching behind his back, into one of his jersey pockets. He pulled out a pistol and began firing it at me.

POP!

POP! POP! POP!

Bullets whizzed past my head and ricocheted off the ground beside my tires. But I kept hammering. So far, I hadn't been hit.

The bullets stopped flying, and I glanced back again to see that Lin Tan had climbed onto his bike. He was coming for me, the pistol still in his hand.

I tried to decide what to do. I could race back to the apartment, but then what? Loo the security guard was there, but I didn't remember seeing him carrying a gun. More than that, Lin Tan was on a road bike, and it was a straight shot over smooth pavement from here back to the apartment. He might catch me before I got there. What would a sneaky, clever jackal do?

I caught sight of the highway and remembered what Loo had said about Old Town. If the roads were as bad as he'd said, Lin Tan's bike would be useless there, whereas I'd be just fine. BMX bikes were designed for rides like that.

I pushed every ounce of energy I could into my thighs and rocketed toward Old Town.

So did Lin Tan. By the time I reached the highway, he was too close for comfort. He raised the pistol and took a couple more shots at me.

POP!

POP! POP!

I put my head down and somehow managed to cross underneath the highway without getting a bullet in my back. The nicely paved road I was riding on came to an abrupt T, and I made a hard left turn onto incredibly uneven pavement. I began to skid, so I drove my left heel into the ground. My shoe bounced and skittered across asphalt that was more uneven than any mountain bike trail I'd ever ridden. Thankfully, I managed to right myself and put my foot back onto my pedal. That really hurt. There was no way Lin Tan would be able to ride a road bike here.

I reached another T-shaped intersection and randomly decided to make a hard right as Lin Tan reached the first gnarly section of road. I heard him cry out, and there was a loud metallic crash as he dumped his bike. If I hadn't been so terrified, I would have laughed out loud. As it was, I continued deeper into Old Town as quickly as possible.

After just one block, however, I had to dismount. I would have been fine continuing to ride this stretch if it were daylight and I was empty-handed, but attempting to ride now in the dark while juggling the large dragon bone container was just too much.

I hurried along, pushing my bike, when I passed in front of a low building with an open front door. The doorway appeared empty, but when I went by, a large hand suddenly shot out of the darkness from behind me and clamped over my mouth. I tried to spin away, but the person's other hand took hold of one of my belt loops and held me fast.

I dropped my bike and tried to elbow my assailant with my free arm, but it was no use. The other person managed to keep me at arm's length like a man holding a snake far away from his body.

I began to grunt out of frustration and effort, and the person who was latched on to me whispered, "Shhhh!"

It wasn't much of a statement, but I could tell that it wasn't Lin Tan's voice. It was too raspy, like the voice of an old man who had smoked far too many cigarettes.

I relaxed, and so did the grip across my mouth. I turned slowly to see the old man who'd watched my tricks from the bike lane. He smiled his toothless grin and motioned for me to come inside. I grabbed my bike and pushed it into the little building. He closed a door behind me.

As far as I could tell, this was the old man's house. It was tiny, to say the least, but it was tidy. It consisted of a single room with no windows, and no bathroom that I could see. There was a small table and two chairs in one corner, and a bed in another corner. On top of the table was a little gas burner with an empty wok as well as a handful of lit candles.

A boy was sitting on the bed. He looked about six or seven years old. I guessed he was the old man's grandson or maybe even his great-grandson. The kid didn't seem at all interested in the fact that his old caregiver had just accosted a foreigner. He was too busy reading a kung fu graphic novel.

The old man pointed to the wok and rubbed his stomach. He was asking if I was hungry. I was, but I didn't want to impose any more than I already was, so I just shook my head and took off my helmet.

The old guy shrugged and pulled a circular bamboo object out of a threadbare bag that he had slung over one shoulder. The object had a diameter of about nine or ten inches, and it looked like a wheel that had been wrapped in newspaper. The old man unwrapped the newspaper, and I saw that there were actually two "wheels" that had been woven together with string. Sandwiched between the wheels were uncooked dumplings. It was some sort of dumpling steamer.

Figured.

The old man lit the small gas burner with one of the candles, then poured some bottled water into the wok. He nested the dumpling steamer against the inner walls of the wok above the water, then pulled a lid from a cupboard and sealed the wok. Some steam still managed to escape the lid, though, and within minutes, the entire room smelled like Chinese food.

Delicious Chinese food.

Whereas the dumplings I'd smelled earlier in the mini-van seemed oily, these did not. They smelled fresh and somehow soupy, probably because they were being steamed with water.

I *loved* soup. My stomach began to growl, and the old man laughed. He rubbed his stomach again, and this time, I nodded.

He seemed pleased. After a few more minutes of steam-ing, the old guy removed the lid. I thought I was going to pass out from the sheer awesomeness of the aroma that bil-lowed forth.

The old man removed three bowls and three sets of chopsticks from the cupboard along with three Chinese soup spoons, which seemed odd to me. He dished five dumplings into each bowl and handed me and the kid on the bed a bowl, a set of chopsticks, and a spoon.

I had no idea how to use the chopsticks, so I just held them and the spoon, and waited to watch and see how the others did it. However, they just stared back at me. It was clear that they wanted me to go first.

I shrugged and set the chopsticks down. I scooped up one of the dumplings with the spoon and popped it half-way into my mouth. The dumpling wasn't all that big, and I could have easily gotten the entire thing in there, but I didn't want to appear greedy. I bit down, and there was a sudden explosion of heat and steam and deliciousness that gushed into my mouth and ran down my chin.

Soup! The dumplings were filled with soup as well as meat! Genius!

I scrambled to catch the meat and as much soup as possible with my spoon before it dribbled off of my chin and onto the floor. It was the best soup I'd ever tasted in my life. Eating it for breakfast might even top huevos rancheros.

The old man and the kid laughed, and the old man looked genuinely happy. He gave me a big thumbs-up, then he and the boy dug into their dumplings, popping each one into their mouths whole. They used their chopsticks to handle the dumplings, but held their spoons at the ready in case any soup attempted to sneak out of their mouths.

I followed their lead, except I used the spoon for every step of the operation. Each time I bit into a dumpling, the same amazing combination of sensations and flavors filled my mouth and splashed over my tongue. I was in heaven.

When I'd finished, I tried to give the old guy some money, but he wouldn't take any. It frustrated me, but at the same time it was obvious that sharing his meal and sheltering me had made him happy, so I let it go. I waited about half an hour more, then decided I should leave. Lin Tan was probably long gone. Since he had fired a gun, though, there were bound to be police officers crawling all over the place.

I motioned toward the door, and the old guy seemed to know what I was planning to do. He shook my hand, then pantomimed that I should wait. I remained seated at his little table while he opened the door and peered outside. He slipped out the door, returning a few minutes later. He flashed me an okay sign, and I stood.

I picked up the upside-down container of dragon bone and frowned. This was going to be a pain to transport.

The old guy snapped his fingers to get my attention, and

he opened the cupboard next to the one that held the eating utensils. He pulled out a roll of duct tape and handed it to me. I patched the crack in the plastic dragon bone container, then I patched my backpack. I put the dragon bone into the pack and tested the pack's strength. It was as good as new.

I handed the duct tape back to the old man and tried to give him some money again, but he still refused.

I grabbed my bike to leave, then realized that I had no idea where I was going. If I went back to the apartment, the police would surely stop me. After all, there were at least a hundred people who'd seen the guy Lin Tan was shooting at. Most of those people had also heard him yell "Dragon bone!" The police would definitely confiscate the substance, canceling out the very reason I'd come to China in the first place.

I thought for a moment about maybe leaving the dragon bone here with the old man, but that was just plain stupid. What I needed to do was head straight to Hú Dié and her dying mother before anybody even knew that I'd left Shanghai. This meant that I probably couldn't take the bike with me. I got the little kid's attention and motioned for him to come to me. He did, and I handed him my bike and the helmet.

I don't think I'd ever seen a happier kid. He squealed with delight, and I looked over at the old man, who appeared as if he was going to cry. I nodded to the old guy, and he bowed. Then he pressed an old baseball cap and a tattered scarf into my hands and shuffled me to the doorway, pointing up the street, away from the direction I'd come. He was thinking the same thing I was thinking, that I needed to mask my identity and skip town.

I pointed in the same direction that he pointed, copying him, and then he gestured right with his arm, then left, and then right again. He was showing me the way out. I mirrored his gestures, and he gave me another thumbs-up.

We shook hands one more time, and I wrapped the scarf around my face and placed the hat on my head.

Then I hurried off into the darkness.

16

Getting out of Old Town was the easy part. Figuring out what to do next proved to be much more difficult.

The opposite side of Old Town was a part of Shanghai that looked exactly the way I imagined a Chinese city would look—lots of crowded tall buildings covered with glowing neon signs and streets spilling over with people. There were no bike lanes here, however, and very few bikes, probably because the traffic was so congested. I couldn't have ridden here even if I'd wanted to.

I walked past dozens of people, and nearly every one of them stared at me. I was beginning to think they all recognized me from the billboards, but then I caught a glimpse of my reflection in a storefront window. I looked ridiculous. What I was wearing was worse than not wearing any disguise at all. I totally looked like I had something to hide. I ditched the scarf and hat in the nearest Dumpster and headed into what I took to be the Shanghai equivalent of a convenience store. It was time for more drastic measures.

I cruised the aisles, grabbing everything I could think of: scissors, black hair wax, surgical masks, cheap sunglasses, a hairbrush, and a pocket mirror. I took the items to the cashier and paid with some of the money Ling had given me.

I walked a couple blocks before I spotted what I needed next. It was a McDonald's. I bypassed the counter and headed straight for the restroom. Luckily, one of the two stalls was empty, and I went inside, locking the flimsy door behind me. I worked as quickly as I could, chopping at my shaggy hair along the sides of my head and flushing the blond clumps down the toilet. Next, I slathered my head with the black hair wax.

I pushed my hair straight up in the center, forming a wicked thick and tall Mohawk. People tended to not stare long at guys who had Mohawks, especially crappy ones like mine.

I put the pocket mirror, scissors, hair wax, and everything else except the sunglasses and a single surgical mask into my backpack alongside the dragon bone. I slipped on the mask and sunglasses and stepped back out into the night.

My disguise worked. People not only didn't stare at me, they went out of their way to avoid me, giving me plenty of space. I even freaked myself out a couple times after catching a glimpse of my reflection in a window. It wasn't so much that I looked mean, it was that I looked *disturbed*. It was mostly because of the hack-job haircut, but the sunglasses added a nice demented touch, too. I'd chosen hot pink frames.

I walked a few more blocks before finding the final item I needed—a prepaid cell phone. As luck would have it, the person behind the counter spoke English just fine, and I spent the rest of the money Ling had given me, plus half of what my parents had given me.

But it was worth it. I left the store and dialed Hú Dié's number, which I had memorized.

"Wai?"

"Hú Dié?" I said through the surgical mask. "It's me."

"Jake!" she said. "Where are you? I do not recognize this number."

"I bought a prepaid cell phone. I'm in Shanghai, but I need to get out of here. Lin Tan is after me."

"Lin Tan? Are you sure? I thought he—"

"I'm positive. Look, I don't really have time to talk about him now. I want to bring the, you know, *stuff* to you. What's the best way for me to do that?"

"I am not sure. I believe I am being watched."

"By whom?"

"I do not know, which makes it a problem. Maybe it is one of Lin Tan's associates?"

"Does he even have associates anymore?"

"I am not sure. My father and I have been under surveillance before, and I am certain it is happening to us again. At least, it is happening to me."

"So I can't come see you?"

"I did not say that. We can still meet. It is just that I need to figure out a safe place. Let me think. . . . Okay, I know a place. It is going to be a little awkward for you to get there, but you can manage. You are clever. I am assuming that you plan to return immediately to Shanghai, yes?"

"No," I said. "I'd rather go straight home, if I can."

"What about the race?" Hú Dié asked.

"I don't think Phoenix and Ryan have gotten the clearance to travel yet. If they can't make it, Mr. Chang is going to make you and me race together as a two-person team against the rest of the field. That includes full adult teams and a new four-person Chinese youth team that he just put together."

"There is another group of kids?"

"Yeah."

"Who are they?"

"I have no idea. I only met one of them, and he's a total nutcase. Ling says he's a great rider, though."

"So you think we should just skip the race because of these things?" Hú Dié asked. "Don't you at least want to give it your best shot? Mr. Chang has not even announced the length of the race yet. If it is a criterium like we rode in California, you and I might do well."

"No thanks," I said. "How long is it going to take me to get to Kaifeng?"

"I am pretty certain there is a bullet train that leaves Shanghai around midnight each day. It would put you in Kaifeng around six-thirty a.m., but I do not think it is wise for us to meet here. After you arrive in Kaifeng, you need to take a long taxi ride to a small village at the edge of a low mountain range. Find a taxi driver who speaks English, and tell him that you want to go to the Tea Village beside the mountains. Every Chinese person in this region knows which village I am talking about. It should cost approximately one hundred US dollars. Can you afford that?"

"Yeah," I said. "That's about seven hundred Chinese yuán. I've got a couple thousand yuán left from a pile of money my parents converted for me. What should I do once I get to the village?"

"Meet me next to the well in the center of the village park. There is only one park and one well. I will be there by noon. You should get there before me."

"Are you sure we need to meet that far from your mother?"

"Yes. Besides, there is something else I would like to show you near there. It would be a shame for you to come all this way and not see it."

"If you say so," I said. "Will I need your help buying a ticket for the bullet train?"

"No. There will be plenty of bullet train ticket sellers who speak English. I do not remember how much it costs, though. Will you have enough money for that, too? I believe they take credit cards."

"I'm fine if they take plastic," I said. "My folks beefed up my credit card. I'd better run."

"Good luck," Hú Dié said. "I once told you that I do not know how I will ever be able to thank you, but I might have just come up with an idea."

"Don't worry about it. Let's just meet and do what I came here to do. Goodbye for now."

"Goodbye, Jake. See you tomorrow."

I ended the call and took a deep breath. It was really

nice talking with Hú Dié again. Maybe everything was going to work out, after all. I still wasn't so sure about racing if it was just the two of us, but I wouldn't put it past myself to change my mind for her. I'd certainly done it before.

I turned off my new cell phone to conserve the battery and scanned the street for a taxi. I needed to get to the station before the last bullet train left for the night.

Six-thirty a.m. came sooner than I'd expected. Perhaps it had something to do with the awesomeness of the bullet train. Now I knew why Phoenix had wanted so badly to ride one.

The superfast train blasted me 575 miles in a little more than six hours, and that included a few stops along the way. It rode smooth as butter, and I slept like a baby the entire ride. Nobody messed with me. The hair and sunglasses were still working their mojo. I was seriously considering keeping them even after I returned home.

When I got out of the train station in Kaifeng, I found a line of empty taxis with eager drivers waiting for customers. I poked my head into half a dozen taxis before I found a driver who spoke enough English to get me where I needed to go. I confirmed the price before I got in and felt kind of proud of myself for haggling down the rate.

As the driver pulled out of the line of taxis, I turned my

cell phone back on. There were no messages. I successfully fought the urge to call Hú Dié, and I settled in for the long drive.

Downtown Kaifeng wasn't too congested at this early hour, but traffic picked up by the time we reached the outskirts of the city. There were no bike lanes here, but the streets teemed with bicycles of all shapes and sizes. Phoenix had told me that he and Hú Dié had ridden through these streets on mountain bikes. I couldn't even begin to imagine how horrible that must have been. Besides the insane drivers who constantly switched lanes without any rhyme or reason while laying on their horns the entire time, nearly every vehicle billowed thick clouds of gray and black exhaust. I put a surgical mask on, even though I was in the backseat of the taxi with the windows closed.

Once we left Kaifeng's limits, the traffic cleared, and so did the air. I even rolled the windows down and took off my mask. It was getting warm outside but not uncomfortable. I was still wearing the same clothes I'd been wearing when I arrived in China, and they were beginning to get a bit funky. I hoped I would get a chance to change into something else soon.

The ramshackle housing on the city's outskirts had given way to farm fields. Open views and the scents of crops filled the taxi. The change of scenery put the taxi driver into a talkative mood, but I played the role of the antisocial, Mohawk-rocking silent type, and didn't engage.

So we ended up driving along in silence, and I soon found myself nodding off to sleep again. I had no idea how frequent international travelers like pilots and flight attendants could handle constant jet lag. It made me sleepy just thinking about it.

I woke to the sensation of the taxi rolling to a stop, and I looked up to see that we were beside a pretty little park in the center of a small but active village. I spotted the old well right away, and reached into my pocket to pay the driver. I handed him seven hundred yuán. When I told him to keep the change, I thought he was going to hug me. My quick scowl sent him leaning backward, though, and I fought back the urge to grin. Ah, the power of the Mohawk.

I got out of the taxi and checked the time on my cell phone. It was nine a.m. I still had three hours to kill, so I decided to walk around.

It was a beautiful little village set at the foot of a fairly tall mountain, with even taller mountains beyond. I noticed almost immediately why this place was called Tea Village. There were tea distributors everywhere. Workers shoveled mounds of dried tea leaves into wooden barrels and fabric sacks before loading them onto flatbed trucks and ox-drawn carts. The village was a cool combination of old-school and new-school ways. I loved it.

My stomach began to growl, and I decided that I should find some food. I didn't have to go far. Directly across the street from the park was a woman selling dumplings out of a cart that was connected to one half of an ancient, rusted bicycle. I couldn't ask for anything more perfect than that.

I bought ten *xiao long bao,* or soup dumplings, I now knew, for the unbelievable price of ten cents each. They were so cheap and so incredibly delicious, I bought ten more. The woman seemed to question my sanity when I bought the other batch, and I didn't blame her. Ten was enough to fill anybody's stomach. Twenty was just plain wrong.

I ate every single one of them.

I'd just polished off the last dumpling when a motorcycle came tearing up the road toward the park. The driver was wearing a complete set of protective leather clothing and a full-faced mirrored shield helmet. The outfit was designed for people who rode street motorcycles, but this was a dirt bike. It was made for riding off-road.

The motorcyclist glanced my way as he passed, then he did a double take and spun the bike around, heading straight for me. My back was against a wall, with the old woman and her cart to my right and a tall stack of tea sacks to my left. I had nowhere to go.

The motorcycle skidded to a stop a few yards from me, and I quickly reached into my pack, pulling out the scissors I'd purchased in Shanghai. They weren't the most intimidating weapon, but they were all I had.

The motorcyclist flipped up his visor and laughed out loud. "Are you really going to defend yourself with that, Jake? You could not even defend your own hair against them! What on earth happened to your head! And why are you wearing *pink* sunglasses?"

The motorcyclist wasn't a guy at all. It was Hú Dié.

I frowned and put the scissors back into my pack. "They both make me look . . . tough."

Hú Dié giggled. "Of course they do. How silly of me. Come over here and give me a hug. I have missed you."

This time hugging her seemed without question like the

right thing to do. It was a little awkward with my sky-high hair and her helmet, but we managed. The old lady who sold me the dumplings looked totally confused by the whole scene, and I couldn't say that I blamed her.

"I have what you've been waiting for," I said with a huge grin, and I began to take my pack off my back.

"Not now," Hú Dié snapped. "Later. I want to take you someplace first."

"Are you sure we have time?"

"Yes. My mother's condition has stabilized. Do you remember Hok mentioning a woman named PawPaw?"

"Sure."

"Well, PawPaw came down from Beijing a few days ago for some other business, but she has been kind enough to stop by and see my mother several times. She is with her now, allowing me a chance to get out of the nursing home for a little while. A ride through the mountains with you is exactly what I want right now. I wish we could be on mountain bikes, but I do not have *that* much time. This motorcycle is the next best thing."

"I didn't know you had a motorcycle."

"I didn't, until Phoenix and I took this one from a former associate of Lin Tan. I just bought this outfit last night after I spoke with you. I found it at a thrift shop, of all places. Do you like it?"

"I guess," I said. "About Lin Tan. We need to talk about him."

"Of course we do, but not right now. Jump on, Jake. I feel the need for speed."

I looked at the tiny section of seat left behind Hú Dié.

There was barely enough room for the battered motorcycle helmet she had strapped there, let alone my butt.

"Are you sure?" I asked. "There doesn't seem to be a whole lot of room back here."

Hú Dié scooted forward five or six inches. "That is the best I can do. Phoenix rode back there before and survived. You will be fine, too. There are foot pegs for your feet, and you can hang on to the sides of the seat where those tie-downs are located. Put that helmet on and let's get moving!"

I groaned and put the helmet on, smashing my spectacular Mohawk. I climbed onto the small section of the hard seat, grabbed hold of the tie-downs, put my feet up, and Hú Dié took off.

We zipped down the village's main street until it ended at a wide dirt trail. Hú Dié shot up the trail with reckless abandon, making me regret having eaten those first ten soup dumplings, let alone the second ten.

Hú Dié drove so fast, the rush of air made me squint even behind my sunglasses. We blasted up, over, and down a series of low mountains, along bumpy terrain, leaving my hands sore and my backside screaming for mercy.

Eventually, we reached a relatively flat stretch of ground in a sort of valley that was filled with overgrown trees. Hú Dié somehow located a narrow trail that looked as if it had been cut by a weed trimmer, and she followed it at break-neck speed to a clearing that ended at a tall stone wall. The wall was crumbling and broken, looking as if it had been brutally attacked many years ago. Hú Dié shot through a gap in the wall and skidded to a stop.

I jumped off the motorcycle, eager to give my aching

bottom a break. I scanned the area, taking everything in. This had to be Cangzhen Temple, the once famous temple where Phoenix's grandfather had lived four hundred years ago. It had been attacked and destroyed back then, and more or less forgotten by history.

I could see why. There was nothing else here. It was in the middle of nowhere. The temple actually consisted of several stone buildings surrounding the courtyard in which we stood. They would need some serious reconstruction to be of use to anyone.

Unless, of course, it were turned into a BMX skills course. In which case, I could see dozens of lines screaming for me to ride them. More than that, the surrounding hills and mountains would be a killer place for mountain bike or BMX trails. The dirt looked perfect.

Hú Dié took off her helmet and shook out her long black hair. It glistened in the sunlight, and a man's deep voice called out, *"Hú Dié?"*

"Grandmaster Long!" Hú Dié cried. "Yes! It is me!"

A very large, very ancient man emerged from a small stone shed. He was broad-shouldered and barrel-chested, and he stood straight as an oak. However, his skin sagged in every direction, and he had massive liver spots all over his bald head. He wore an orange monk's robe and managed to look both menacing and kind at the same time. He bowed to me.

I bowed back. Bowing was cool.

"I have brought a friend," Hú Dié said. "I believe you may have heard of him. His name is Jake. He is the one who got Phoenix interested in mountain bikes."

"Greetings, Jake," he said. "I am Grandmaster Long. Welcome to Cangzhen Temple."

"A pleasure to make your acquaintance, sir." I bowed again, this time as low as I possibly could. I remembered reading one time that this was the ultimate show of respect to elders.

Hú Dié giggled. "No need to be so formal, Jake. It would be a shame for you to put your back out bowing so low."

I frowned and straightened up.

Grandmaster Long smiled. "I see nothing wrong with the gesture, Hú Dié. In fact, I appreciate it, Jake. It has been too long since someone afforded me the respect I feel I deserve."

"No problem, sir," I said.

"Why are you here?"

"Um . . . ," I said.

"Jake is in town for a bike race, and I needed to get out of the house, so we decided to go on a little joyride. Isn't that right, Jake?"

"Yeah, that's right." I looked at Grandmaster Long. "This is a very . . . interesting place. How long have you lived here?"

"Longer than you can imagine, but it seems that time has come to an end. I once had the foolish notion that I could rebuild this special place. Alas, I have decided to give up. I have rented an apartment next door to my old friend, PawPaw, in Beijing. I will be moving very soon."

Hú Dié looked like she was going to cry. "No! You can't do that. It wouldn't be right."

"Everything has its time," Grandmaster Long said.

"This is true for people as well as places. Some things have changed in my world, and I have new priorities. I am very glad you have come, though. I still have something that belongs to you inside the weapons shed."

"Trixie!" Hú Dié cried, and she climbed off the motorcycle. She ran into the shed from which Grandmaster Long had just appeared, and a moment later she came out pushing the craziest-looking pink mountain bike I'd ever seen. Where there were usually shocks, the bike had rigid frame welds. Where there were usually welds, the bike had shocks. Strangest of all, the bike had no seat or seat post.

Hú Dié beamed. "Jake, meet Trixie, my custom mountain bike. What do you think?"

"I think she's totally whacked," I replied. "By that I mean both you *and* your bike. Nobody names their ride."

"Sure they do," she said. "I—"

Hú Dié stopped suddenly and cocked her head to one side as if listening. I heard the whine of an engine.

"Oh, no!" Hú Dié said. "Not again!"

"What?" I asked.

"Lin Tan—"

Grandmaster Long laughed and laid a hand on Hú Dié's arm. "No, Hú Dié. Relax. It's not Lin Tan."

"Are you sure?" she asked.

"Positive," he replied.

"Who is it, then?"

"It is PawPaw," Grandmaster Long said. "She is coming to get me. I've been rather weak the past few days, and she planned to rent some sort of all-terrain vehicle so that I won't have to make the long walk all the way to the Tea Village before hiring a taxi. I wasn't expecting her for another day or two, but perhaps the vehicle was unavailable then."

"But you didn't say why it is that you're positive it isn't Lin Tan," Hú Dié said.

"Lin Tan is dead," Grandmaster Long replied. "I thought you would have heard this by now."

I felt my eyes widen, and Hú Dié pulled her arm from beneath Grandmaster Long's hand.

"He's still *alive!*" I said. "Lin Tan attacked me in Shanghai yesterday, and now he's following me!"

"Lin Tan is alive?" Grandmaster Long asked, still not believing me.

A small dune buggy suddenly zipped through the gap in the wall, and there wasn't an old woman behind the wheel.

It was Lin Tan.

Hú Dié dropped Trixie and raced into the weapons shed, followed closely by Grandmaster Long. I didn't know the first thing about kung fu weapons, so I ran over to Trixie and climbed onto the crazy mountain bike as Lin Tan veered toward me.

Trixie's pedals were clipless, which meant that you needed clips on the bottoms of your shoes to clip into them. I wasn't wearing mountain biking shoes, so I couldn't clip in, but Trixie's pedals were egg-beater style and fairly wide, so at least I could get a little purchase. I sped away as best I could just as Lin Tan ran over the very spot where Trixie and I had been half a second earlier.

Hú Dié howled like a banshee and came running out of the shed with a wide three-foot-long sword attached to the end of a six-foot staff. Grandmaster Long came out carrying one, too. I knew that the weapon was called a *kwan dao,* but only because of *Teenage Mutant Ninja Turtles.*

Hú Dié howled again, and Lin Tan spun his vehicle around. He wasn't wearing a helmet, and I saw that he was as bald as Grandmaster Long, except his scalp was as black and scaly as his face. He sped toward Hú Dié—and as he was about to plow into her, she leaped high into the air, swinging the *kwan dao*'s blade straight down.

Hú Dié cleared the steel roll cage that crisscrossed the top of the dune buggy, and the blade headed straight for Lin Tan's bald black head. Unfortunately, the blade nicked one of the roll cage's crossbars, and the weapon bounced straight back up at Hú Dié.

She released it in midair, and both she and the *kwan dao* went down hard on the courtyard's paving stones.

Lin Tan cut his steering wheel and headed toward Grandmaster Long. The old man sidestepped the dune buggy like a matador avoiding a charging bull and stabbed his massive blade into the opening where there would normally be a driver's side door.

However, the dune buggy was traveling too fast. The blade clanged off the door frame before it could connect with Lin Tan, and the weapon was wrenched from Grandmaster Long's hands.

Lin Tan turned his vehicle back toward Hú Dié.

She was on her knees, attempting to stand. Her fall had really knocked her for a loop. There was no way she was going to be able to jump over the dune buggy again. I aimed Trixie for a head-on collision with Lin Tan and pedaled the bizarre seatless mountain bike with all my might. I swerved in front of Hú Dié and shouted, *"Move!"*

Hú Dié leaped sideways while I continued straight toward Lin Tan. I saw him smirk, and when I was certain a collision was inevitable, I bunny-hopped with all my strength while laying the bike sideways in a tabletop maneuver.

I kicked the bike away from me while twisting to one side, sending Trixie spinning toward the windshieldless dune buggy. The force of my kick spun me around the side of the vehicle, and I managed to avoid contact with the buggy altogether.

Lin Tan wasn't so lucky with Trixie. As I hit the ground, I saw one end of the mountain bike's sturdy handlebars sink deep into his right temple.

The dune buggy suddenly lost speed and slowly rolled to a stop. Lin Tan's dead foot must have slipped off of the gas pedal.

Hú Dié was standing now, and she wobbled over to me as Grandmaster Long ran over to Lin Tan with his enormous *kwan dao* back in his hands. The old man tossed Trixie aside and turned off the dune buggy's engine. He unfastened the seat belt and dragged Lin Tan's limp body out of the vehicle.

"Is he—?" Hú Dié asked.

Grandmaster Long nodded. "Yes. He won't be bothering you or anyone else ever again. Well done, Jake."

I turned away and puked twenty soup dumplings all over the courtyard.

A few minutes later, Hú Dié rested a hand on my back and said, "I am so proud of you, Jake. You saved my life."

"I believe you saved both our lives," Grandmaster Long said. "I'm not the man I used to be. I don't think I could have stopped Lin Tan. You both saw me try, and fail."

I shook my head. "Stop it, you two. Let me puke in peace."

Grandmaster Long laughed. "Your reaction shows that you do not condone violence. That is an admirable trait, Jake. Let me bring you something to drink. Perhaps a—"

A cell phone suddenly rang, and Hú Dié jumped. She hurriedly unzipped one of the pockets in her leather riding jacket and pulled out her phone. She looked at the screen, and her face went pale.

"Who is it?" I asked.

"It's my mother's number, but she can no longer speak. She has lost control of her vocal cords."

"Answer it," Grandmaster Long said. "It may be PawPaw."

Hú Dié answered the phone. *"Wai?"*

She said nothing for a few seconds, then she seemed to relax. "Okay," she said, "see you soon." And she handed the phone to Grandmaster Long. "It is PawPaw. She is calling for you."

Grandmaster Long didn't look surprised. He spoke with PawPaw in Chinese for what seemed like forever before hanging up the phone and handing it back to Hú Dié.

"I guess I had better get back to my mother's nursing home."

Grandmaster Long nodded. "I am going, too." He jerked his chin toward Lin Tan's dune buggy. "I will drive that. Jake can ride with me. You can ride the motorcycle."

"Is anybody planning on telling me what's going on?" I asked.

"PawPaw is heading to the Kaifeng airport to pick up Hok," Grandmaster Long said, "along with a few other visitors. We will meet them at the nursing home."

"Hok is *here*?"

"That is what I just said."

"Sorry, Jake," Hú Dié said. "I should have mentioned her coming earlier when I told you about PawPaw. Hok is supposed to bring additional herbs to add to the ones Paw-Paw has been giving my mother."

"PawPaw is *treating* your mother?" I asked, clutching my backpack. "I thought she was just evaluating her or something. What about the . . . you know?"

"Dragon bone?" Grandmaster Long asked.

My eyes widened.

"Don't be so shocked," Grandmaster Long said. "Phoenix realized yesterday what you'd done. He'd already told his grandfather, Hok, PawPaw, and me about the extra dragon bone that he hid. Even if Phoenix hadn't said a word, I would have guessed that your sudden appearance here has something to do with dragon bone. Why else would you be here? More than that, why else would Lin Tan have followed you? My guess is that you have Phoenix's dragon bone in your bag."

My grip loosened on my backpack. "So much for me being a sneaky jackal. Phoenix is going to hate me forever."

"You might be surprised," Grandmaster Long said. "You simply did what he planned to do anyway. In fact, he feels quite bad for not having acted sooner."

Hú Dié gasped. "You mean Phoenix decided to give me some dragon bone for my mother, after all?"

Grandmaster Long nodded. "Except, by the time he had convinced his grandfather to drive him to the trail to retrieve it, the police had arrived at their home to question both Phoenix and Ryan about the accidental mountain biking death of a Chinese gangster from California at the very same state park."

"DaXing," I said.

"Yes," Grandmaster Long said. "Phoenix had a hunch that you may have been involved, but he said nothing to the police."

I felt my cheeks begin to blush. "Guilty as charged," I said. "Hú Dié told me how I could find Phoenix's stash. I took a limo to the state park the same day she left. DaXing must have followed me. He attacked me after I found the dragon bone, and I took off on my bike. He fell into a ravine when he was chasing me. His death really was an accident."

"Regardless," Grandmaster Long said, "I have to say, I am glad that it was you who took it and not someone who might have used the substance for questionable purposes, especially with DaXing being there. Once the police were satisfied that Phoenix and Ryan had in no way been harboring DaXing, nor were they responsible for his death, they said that the boys were free to travel here. So they did."

"Phoenix and Ryan are in China now, too?" I asked. "In Shanghai?"

Grandmaster Long shook his head. "Mr. Chang could not arrange a flight to Shanghai on such short notice for Phoenix, his grandfather, Ryan, and Ryan's mother. So the four of them flew to Beijing, and then on to Kaifeng. Their plane just landed. Hok was on the same flight from Beijing to Kaifeng. They are the others that I had mentioned were traveling with Hok."

"Mr. Chang arranged their flights?" Hú Dié asked.

"All of the flights except for Hok's. He knows nothing about her. Mr. Chang agreed to pay the others' way to Kaifeng because they can take the midnight bullet train from there to Shanghai. There weren't enough airplane or train seats available to get them from Beijing directly to Shanghai in time for the big race tomorrow morning."

"Mr. Chang still wants us to race?" I asked.

Grandmaster Long nodded. "He has been in constant contact with Ryan's mother and Phoenix's grandfather. He has been worried about you, Jake. PawPaw just told me that she will get word to Mr. Chang through Ryan's mother about you having surfaced here at Cangzhen Temple. Ryan's mother will contact your parents, too. Once everyone has been informed that you are fine, I am certain they will all be eager to see you and Hú Dié race alongside Phoenix and Ryan tomorrow."

"I'm sorry," I said. "I didn't mean to make so many people worry."

"All's well that ends well," Grandmaster Long said.

I hefted my backpack. "I can't believe I've done all this for nothing."

"On the contrary," Grandmaster Long said. "Your drastic actions were the catalyst for something much bigger."

"Huh?"

Grandmaster Long smirked. "You will learn more when we arrive in Kaifeng."

18

We pulled into the nursing home parking lot just after sunset. We were a sorry-looking bunch, Hú Dié, Grandmaster Long, and me. Hú Dié said not to worry about it. Her mother had a private room, and she wouldn't care how much dirt and road grime covered us. She was used to seeing Hú Dié covered head to toe in bicycle grease.

Hú Dié's mother's room was packed with people. Waiting for us were Phoenix, his grandfather, Ryan, Ryan's mom, and Hok, along with Hú Dié's mother and an old woman I'd never met but was certainly PawPaw.

Hú Dié's mother was lying in bed, covered to her neck with blankets. Her skin was snow-white, and her head shook terribly. Even so, her eyes were perfectly clear.

They were Hú Dié's eyes.

Hú Dié pushed her way through the group and kissed her mother on the cheek. Hú Dié said a few words in Chinese, and her mother gave a shaky nod of her head. I felt so bad for Hú Dié's mom. Any trace of regret I might have had about bringing the dragon bone here vanished. No one should have to go through what Hú Dié's mother was experiencing.

Not surprisingly, Ryan's mom took control of the room. "Well, the gang's all here," she said. "First things first. Jake, what in heaven's name happened to your *hair*?"

I pushed my dirt-streaked black Mohawk out of my face. "It's a long story. I'll tell everybody later. We have more important things to talk about right now." I turned to Phoenix. "How've you been, bro?"

Phoenix shrugged. "I don't know. Good and bad. Mostly good now, though. You?"

"Same," I said. "I, uh, heard that you figured out what I did with your dragon bone."

"Yeah. As soon as the police told me that DaXing had had an accident out at the state park, I put two and two together. Were you hurt?"

"No, I'm fine. Are you mad? I understand if you hate me."

Phoenix shook his head. "I don't hate you, but I am angry. It wasn't cool to go behind my back."

"I know. Everything was happening so fast. I'm sorry."

"You should be," Phoenix's grandfather said. "Lucky for you, things may have worked out for the best, though."

"Really?" I asked.

Phoenix nodded. "Do you have the dragon bone?"

I pulled off my backpack. "Right here, bro." I unzipped the pack and handed the container to him. "Watch out for the duct tape."

Phoenix took the container carefully, as if it were filled

with liquid gold. I thought he was going to hand it to Hú Dié's mother, but instead he offered it to Hú Dié.

"Here," Phoenix said. "I'm very sorry that I didn't help you sooner."

Hú Dié took it with trembling hands. "Thank you," she said. "Truly. Thank you, too, Jake."

Phoenix and I nodded.

Hú Dié turned to Hok, PawPaw, Grandmaster Long, and Phoenix's grandfather, who were huddled together in one corner of the room. "May I?"

"You can try," PawPaw said, "but I don't think your mother is interested."

Hú Dié looked confused.

"I explained the substance to her earlier," PawPaw said. "As you know, your mother's physical faculties are limited, but her mind is sharp as a tack. I don't think she wants anything to do with dragon bone. She is a wise woman. Go ahead and offer it, though. It's the least you could do, since Jake has gone through so much trouble bringing it here."

Hú Dié turned to her mother, and her mother suddenly spoke in a hoarse whisper. "Thank you, my love, but no."

Hú Dié nearly dropped the dragon bone. "You can speak!"

Hú Dié's mother nodded and the hint of a smile twitched across her lips.

"It seems the herbs I've been giving her are doing some good," PawPaw said.

"This is amazing," Ryan's mother said. "I had a great-aunt who succumbed to ALS. Is your treatment widely known?"

"I don't believe so," PawPaw said. "The Chinese herbs

I'm using are quite rare. I wouldn't blame any physician for not knowing about them. I have even higher hopes for the herbs Hok has brought. Perhaps we will share our findings with the medical community. These herbs will never repair all of the ALS damage, of course, but I am certain Hú Dié's mother will continue to improve. She will outlive Hok and me, that's for sure."

Hú Dié grinned. Then she suddenly frowned.

I frowned, too. "What do you mean?"

PawPaw smiled. "Hok and I are now free of dragon bone. Our life spans are finite, as nature intended. The same is true for Grandmaster Long and—"

"My grandfather," Phoenix said.

"The antidote!" I said.

Phoenix nodded. "Thankfully, Hok and PawPaw believe that my grandfather will live a lot more than ten years. It's all because of you, Jake."

"Me?" I asked. "How?"

"After DaXing was found," Phoenix's grandfather said, "I called Hok to give her the news about his demise and to tell her of our suspicion—that you had taken the hidden dragon bone to give to Hú Dié's mother. Hok and I decided that enough was enough. We discussed the antidote that she'd concocted that helped Ryan and several others break dragon bone's bonds; and even though she did not believe she would survive the antidote, she took it upon herself to try it anyway. As you can see, it worked. We called Paw-Paw, and she made a batch here in China for her and Long. It worked for them, too. I have wanted to break my bonds with dragon bone for more years than you could possibly imagine, so I had Hok express-mail me the antidote right before we came here. I drank it moments before we left the house. That was yesterday. Like the others, I feel a bit weak, but otherwise, I am fine. More than that, I am truly happy. Hok and PawPaw believe that we all have the constitution of sixty-year-olds. We each expect to live at least another twenty years."

"I can't believe what I'm hearing," I said. "This is so great! What are you going to do with the rest of the dragon bone? I really hate that stuff."

"We're going to dump every last bit into the Yellow River," Hok said. "It's less than a block away. We've all brought our remaining supplies with us."

I turned to Grandmaster Long. "That's what you loaded into the dune buggy before we left the temple."

He nodded.

Hú Dié held out the container of dragon bone she'd been holding, offering it to Phoenix's grandfather. "I apologize for all the trouble I have caused you and your family," she said.

Phoenix's grandfather accepted the dragon bone. "I appreciate that, Hú Dié. Come, let us dump this together. Afterward, we have a bullet train to catch."

I felt my ears perk up. "The race! We're going to do it?"

"I am," Phoenix said. "That is, if everyone else still wants to do it."

"I'm in," Ryan said. "I didn't come all this way for nothing."

"Heck, yeah," I said. "I'm in, too, as long as there's room for me on the train."

"There's plenty of room for all of us," Ryan's mom said. "I've already checked."

I realized that Hú Dié hadn't said anything. Phoenix, Ryan, and I turned to her. She was gazing at her mother.

Hú Dié sighed. "I do not know, guys. My mother is still—"

"Oh, no you don't!" Hú Dié's mother said in a sharp whisper. "You will not remain here on my account. Bicycle racing is your dream. You have the opportunity to realize it. You are going to Shanghai tonight! PawPaw will stay with me."

Hú Dié smiled through the tears that were forming in her eyes. "I guess I am in, too. Somebody had better call Ling and Mr. Chang right away to let them know that they need to bring our bikes and all of our gear to the race."

"I'll do it," Ryan's mom said. "You all go on and get rid of that dragon bone. By the time you return, I hope to have taken care of our bullet train tickets as well."

Phoenix grinned. "Bullet train. Awesome."

We arrived at the race location in downtown Shanghai at 7:30 a.m. the next day, as planned. Everyone came along from Kaifeng except for Hú Dié's mother and PawPaw. Fortunately, it turned out that the race had become such a big deal, it was being broadcast throughout China instead of just locally in Shanghai. Hú Dié's mother and PawPaw would be able to watch the whole thing on television.

We found Ling, who was with a team of mechanics dedicated solely to us four. It was pretty incredible. The mechanics took our measurements and adjusted everyone's bike except Hú Dié's. She insisted on adjusting hers herself.

Once the bikes were done, we changed into our racing kits and gathered together for a group picture. The new uniform felt awesome against my skin, mostly because it was the first set of fresh clothes I'd put on since I'd arrived in China.

Several young girls in the crowd giggled and snapped

our pictures, and Ryan's mom snapped a couple shots, too, but then she suddenly stopped. I turned around to see somebody photobombing us.

It was Keng, the skinny psycho from the Mr. Chang's other youth team. "Hello, fellow teammates!"

"Get lost, freak," I said.

"Look who's calling whom a freak," Keng said. "Nice hair."

I frowned. He actually had a point. We'd gotten club cars with bathrooms on the bullet train, and I'd been able to wash all of the black wax out of my hair. However, it now looked like I had a fat, blond dachshund lying on top of my head.

Keng leaned close to Hú Dié. "Hey, honey. Long time, no see."

"Leave me alone, Keng," she replied. "We are done."

I stared at Hú Dié in disbelief. "You know this guy?"

"Know her?" Keng said. "I *dated* her!"

"I would not call it that," Hú Dié said, and turned to me. "Keng lives near my bike shop, and we went to a couple races together. He is good on a road bike, but useless on a mountain bike."

Keng's beady eyes gleamed. "Good thing for me this is a road bike race."

Phoenix opened his mouth to say something, but then he closed it again. I noticed that his hands were balled into fists.

Keng looked at him. "Hey, I remember you! You are the guy who likes to kick guys like me in the groin, right? We are going to have fun out there today, pal. Count on it."

"*You* attacked *me* in Kaifeng last month!" Phoenix said. "I was minding my own business when you tried to steal my backpack!"

"So you say," Keng said with a dismissive wave of his hand. "I do not have time for this. I have a race to win." He walked off.

Phoenix stared at Hú Dié with the same disbelieving look I probably still had on my face.

"You actually *dated* that slimeball?" Phoenix asked.

"We *raced* together," she replied, "not dated. But even if I did date him, so what?"

"Never mind," Phoenix said, and looked away.

Hú Dié nodded. "That is what I thought. Mind your own business, Phoenix, and put your opinions aside until after the race. We need to be focused."

"Here, here!" Ryan's mom said. "Get focused and stay focused, gang. I think this is going to be a short race."

"How short?" I asked.

"It hasn't been officially announced yet, but there are rumors of it being a criterium. I can't believe Mr. Chang hasn't released the race details yet. I've never heard of such a thing. This clearly isn't a sanctioned race, but no matter. It is what it is. You can't afford to let your minds wander."

"No way," Ryan said. "Look who's coming."

I turned to see SaYui, or *Shark*, headed our way. He used to work for DuSow, and he also raced against us in California. With him were Lucas and Philippe, two Frenchmen who had also raced against us in California and worked for DuSow. Hok's dragon bone antidote had saved all three of them from certain death, which converted them from our enemies to instant compatriots.

"Hello, friends!" SaYui said.

"Yes, bonjour!" Lucas and Philippe said as one.

"Hi, guys," Ryan said. "We didn't know you were going to be here."

"Mr. Chang wanted to keep it a surprise," SaYui said. "He thought it would be fun for us to race alongside you again since we went so close to the wire last time."

"Mr. Chang is full of surprises," I said, "but I don't mind. We beat you once; we'll do it again." I winked.

SaYui laughed.

Ryan's mom cleared her throat. "Nice seeing you guys again, but I'm afraid you're going to have to leave the kids alone now. You're welcome to come back after the race to chat."

"Of course," SaYui said. "We mean no harm. We will see you at the end of the race, when perhaps one of you is on the podium! Best of luck!"

"Best of luck!" I shouted back, and I grabbed my new road bike. Ryan's mom made us do some warm-up drills on stationary trainers that Ling had brought, and then we cooled down. I was feeling pretty good. I'd rather have been on a BMX bike or even a mountain bike, but this was fine. My friends were happy, and that made me happy. They looked all rested, too. We'd talked a bit on the train, catching each other up with what happened with Lin Tan and all that, but we'd spent most of the time getting some shut-eye, which was key. Jet lag was at the front of everyone's minds, and we hoped it wouldn't play a role in the race today.

At ten a.m. sharp, we lined up with the other riders and strapped on our helmets as we listened to the rules. It was going to be a closed-course criterium through select streets here in downtown Shanghai, just like the race in California had been, except this one was taking place in daylight. We would race around a three-mile loop for an hour, at which time a bell would sound to indicate that there was to be one final lap. Whoever crossed the finish line first without being lapped would be declared the winner.

"Riders ready!"

"Here we go!" Ryan said excitedly.

"Take your mark!"

"Let's show them who deserves to be on a billboard!" I shouted.

BANG!

The starter pistol fired, and we were off.

We started in the front row, but so did Keng's team and SaYui's team. The starting line was very wide, so there was plenty of room for us all, but it meant that none of us had any excuses. If we won, it was simply because we were better than the others.

My teammates and I formed the familiar peloton, or line, that we'd drilled for weeks in California. Ryan rode in the lead position, blocking much of the wind for the rest of us with his wide, powerful body. Phoenix rode behind him, followed by Hú Dié and then me. In a normal road race lasting several hours, we would rotate every few minutes, each of us taking turns in the lead. However, in a short race like this, we'd let Ryan pull until his legs gave out. Then he'd fall off to the end of the line and hang on until either his strength returned or he simply stopped trying to keep up with us.

This team approach meant that Ryan wouldn't win the race, but neither would Hú Dié or I. Phoenix was our designated sprinter, and it was everybody else's job to keep his legs as fresh as possible for the final sprint to the finish line. He'd burned up too much of his energy too early in the California race, and Hú Dié and I had passed him. I doubted he'd make the same mistake today.

Our team took the early lead out front, blasting along Shanghai's closed-off streets, but I soon heard people pulling up behind me as I was riding caboose. It was Keng's team. Keng was in the number two position, just like Phoenix. It didn't surprise me. I did my best to ignore their entire team as their lead rider latched on to my rear wheel, which allowed him and his entire team to be pulled partially along by me, in my slipstream. It wasn't the least bit illegal, and professional teams did it all the time. Sometimes there were more than a hundred riders in a single peloton. The trouble was, the more riders you had drafting off of one another, the more likely there was to be an accident, usually a large one. Keng's lead teammate clearly knew that, because he purposely bumped his front tire against my back tire five times in an effort to throw me off balance.

"Yo!" I shouted. "Step off! You don't want a piece of me!"

"What's wrong?" Hú Dié asked from in front of me.

"Keng's lead knucklehead is bumping my back tire."

Hú Dié said something in Chinese that sounded a lot like cursing, and she shouted, "Falling off!"

"What?" I said.

Hú Dié pulled out of our line and stopped pedaling, slowing until her front wheel was in line with the back of mine. I sped up and latched my front tire to Phoenix's rear tire, which should have left plenty of room for Hú Dié to slide in behind me. However, Keng's entire team began to speed up, closing off the space that Hú Dié clearly planned to occupy.

Hú Dié wasn't having any of it. She cut her front wheel in front of Keng's lead rider, and the lead rider freaked out. He obviously hadn't expected her to do that. He swerved to avoid Hú Dié's front tire, and he slammed into a hay-bale barrier wall that had been constructed around the entire course for situations just like this. Keng swerved expertly around his fallen lead rider, and the two guys behind Keng swerved successfully as well.

Keng's team's swerving slowed them a bit, and SaYui's team pulled up next to them.

"Is your guy all right?" SaYui asked Keng.

"Who cares?" Keng replied. "He deserved what he got. Rookie mistake. He has no business riding with us."

"That's pretty harsh," SaYui said. "Do you think that you are a pro now, kid?"

"Sure," Keng said. "Watch." He got out of his saddle and began to sprint, pulling ahead of SaYui and letting SaYui latch on to his rear wheel.

"Impressive," SaYui said in a sarcastic tone. "Let's see you do that forty-five minutes from now."

"Why wait forty-five minutes when we can test one another's skills right now?" Keng said, and slammed on his brakes.

SaYui plowed into the back of Keng's bike.

And Lucas plowed into the back of SaYui's bike.

And Philippe plowed into the back of Lucas's bike.

And Philippe, Lucas, and SaYui all went down in a heap.

Keng's bike swerved wildly, but he managed to just barely steer clear of the barriers and regain control of his bike. That was the most insane move I'd ever seen anyone do on a road bike. Somebody could have gotten killed. As far as I could tell, SaYui and his teammates were still alive, though they all likely suffered broken bones.

"Yee-haw!" Keng whooped. "Isn't that what those Yankee boyfriends of yours shout when they are excited about something, Hú Dié?"

She didn't reply.

I heard Ryan begin to puff like a steam engine up front, and we began to pick up speed. Keng slowed and pulled in between his two remaining teammates behind us.

"Did you see that?" I asked Phoenix. "That Keng kid is out of his mind."

"I saw," Phoenix said. "Let him try that garbage with me."

"I think Hú Dié may get to him before you," I said.

"I heard that!" Hú Dié said. "You are right, Jake. I have your back if he tries to pull anything against us."

We zoomed past the start/finish line, having completed one full lap. Keng's team had lost one rider, and SaYui had lost his entire team. At this rate, there wouldn't be any riders left by the end of the race.

Ryan kept us going at a blistering pace, and the crowd seemed to appreciate it. Most of the people watching the race were concentrated at the start/finish line, and every time we passed and were still in the lead, they cheered louder. Things continued really well until a full fifty minutes into the race, when Ryan shouted, "Falling . . . off!"

The poor kid hardly had enough air left to complete the sentence. He was completely spent, and it was no wonder. He'd pulled us so fast for so long, we'd lapped more than half of the other teams, and they were all adults.

Ryan pulled out of our line, and Keng's team took this as their opportunity to strike. They rushed forward, still in their peloton, and their lead rider latched his tire on to the back of Hú Dié's rear tire.

Ryan was blocked out.

Hú Dié began to slow, forcing Keng's team back, while Phoenix saw what was happening and began to hammer in front of me. I hammered as well, and we opened up a nice space for Ryan between the back of my rear tire and the front of Hú Dié's front tire.

But it was all wasted effort on our part. Ryan was toast. "Sorry . . . guys," he huffed. "I'm . . . done."

"Don't quit!" Hú Dié cried.

"I . . . won't," Ryan said. "I just can't . . . run with . . . you big dogs . . . anymore."

"You're the biggest dog in the pound!" I shouted. "You pulled us like crazy for fifty minutes! We're going to win this for you!"

"Thanks," Ryan managed to huff, and he began to slow until he was out of sight.

"Very touching!" Keng shouted from behind us. "I think it is about time we got this party started." He pulled out from behind his lead rider and began to sprint. When he neared Hú Dié, she swerved in front of him, trying to make him swerve out of control, but he easily avoided her aggressive maneuver.

"I was expecting that, pretty girl," Keng said, blowing her a kiss. "Now stay in the back of the train where you belong." He sprinted again, passing Hú Dié. The kid might be as skinny as a toothpick and as nutty as a chestnut tree, but he was *strong*.

Phoenix began to pick up speed in front of me, and I shouted, "Fall off, Phoenix! Let me pull you to the finish."

"No, I got this," he replied. "There's not much time left."

"Don't be stupid," I said. "Fall off!"

"If you want to be ahead of me so badly, pass me," Phoenix said.

What an idiot, I thought. *Well, it takes one to know one.*

I pulled outside of Phoenix and began to sprint as we crossed over the start/finish line yet again. This time, a bell sounded, and the crowd roared. Just one more lap, and it was over.

I hammered with everything I had and managed to pull ahead of Phoenix.

Keng was off to the side and slightly behind my stubborn best friend.

"Very nice sprint, Jake," Keng said. "Perhaps you should have remained in Phoenix's slipstream until the final straightaway."

I wanted to reply with something sarcastic and clever,

but I didn't have the breath for it. My lungs were now burning as much as my legs. Sprinting ahead of Phoenix was incredibly stupid, but it was his best chance to win. I didn't care about becoming China's poster child for cycling, but Phoenix did. So did Ryan and Hú Dié. Ryan had already made his mark. There were cameras positioned all around the course, and more than a billion people had had the opportunity to watch him pull his team for nearly the entire race. Any cycling team on the planet would be happy to have him, especially since he was only fifteen years old.

As for Hú Dié, she could obviously hang with adult guys. More than that, put her on a mountain bike against any man, woman, or child on the planet and she'd emerge victorious. She could write her own ticket as well.

But Phoenix, he absolutely had to win this race. I wasn't about to let him beat himself by burning out too fast like he always did.

Keng began to pick up speed until he was neck and neck with Phoenix. I expected him to throw a punch or kick or something at Phoenix, but he didn't. Instead, he just rode beside Phoenix, staring at him with those beady eyes.

We rounded a curve, and I realized that we'd already ridden three-fourths of the final lap. We were *flying*. I needed to do something to tire Keng out. Fast.

I looked over at him and huffed, "Hey . . . Keng! Why are you . . . pacing Phoenix? I'm . . . the one to beat!"

Keng laughed. "You cannot even breathe, Jake! Give me a break."

I ground my teeth and willed my legs to push harder. I imagined I was propelling myself up the world's tallest

BMX ramp, where I needed to reach maximum speed or risk coming up short on the far end of the jump. In a lot of ways, it was the perfect analogy.

I felt my speed increase, and I heard Keng laugh again. "Well, what do you know?" he said. "I guess I have been dancing with the wrong partner, after all. Let's see what you have, blondie!"

I continued to push with every ounce of strength I had, keeping my mind focused on that imaginary BMX ramp, blocking out everything else.

I heard Keng groan and noticed that his speed increased just a hair.

But only a hair.

He was riding beside me on my left, and I risked a glance behind. Phoenix was still latched on to my rear wheel, being pulled along in my slipstream. He was breathing hard, but I'd heard him in much worse condition before. I smiled around my open mouth. This was going to work.

Phoenix and I locked eyes, and I nodded my head ever so slightly to my right. Phoenix nodded back.

I began to slowly veer to my left, toward Keng. He was breathing very hard, and his eyes were glued to the road directly in front of him. He was in *the zone*. A bomb could go off beside his head and he wouldn't notice.

I heard the crowd roar and saw that it was time for Phoenix to make his move.

"Now!" I shouted, and Phoenix veered to his right. It would be a tight squeeze between me and the hay bales bordering that side of the course, but he could just make it if he was careful.

I continued to give everything I had, but there wasn't much left. I felt myself begin to slow as Keng continued to drive forward at his blistering pace. He was approaching the start/finish line at a nearly incomprehensible speed.

But Phoenix was going faster.

I stared openmouthed as Phoenix absolutely *blew* past Keng to finish more than a bike length ahead of him. I'd seen it for myself but still couldn't believe it. I'd never seen anybody finish with such authority. I couldn't have been prouder of Phoenix.

The crowd erupted with cheers like I'd never heard, and as I stopped pedaling to coast to a third-place finish, somebody blew past *me*.

It was Hú Dié!

She wailed like a banshee as she crossed the finish line, temporarily stealing some of Phoenix's limelight.

I rolled across the finish line with an entire field of adult men hot on my tail. I steered as best I could toward Phoenix and Hú Dié, who were hugging one another. It was great to see.

Keng was nowhere in sight.

I joined Phoenix and Hú Dié in a group hug, and we turned to watch Ryan pedal across the finish line. He hadn't quit, and he was far from last. Many professionals who'd done what he had done would be in the back of an ambulance by now, sucking on an oxygen bottle.

Phoenix, Hú Dié, and I abandoned our bikes and pushed our way through the cyclists to meet up with Ryan. His head hung low, and Hú Dié punched him in the arm.

Hard.

That got his attention.

"Hey!" he shouted. "What was that for?"

"For being awesome!" she replied, and she kissed him on the cheek. His already red face turned the color of a ripe apple.

"Heck yeah, bro!" I said. "You da man!"

"You sure are," Phoenix said. "We couldn't have done it without you!"

"Done what?" Ryan asked. "I was too far back to see the end of the race. What happened?" He looked at me expectantly. "Did you win?"

"Nope," I said proudly. "Phoenix and Hú Dié both beat me. Phoenix took first, and Hú Dié took third."

"All right!" Ryan shouted, and he bumped fists with both of them. "Did Keng take second?"

"Yeah," I said. "I came crawling in a measly fourth."

"You beat me," Ryan said, "but I don't care. At least one of my teammates won."

"That's the spirit, Ryan!"

I looked over to see that it was Ling who had shouted that. He and Mr. Chang were pushing their way through the crowd toward us. Behind them were Ryan's mom, Phoenix's grandfather, Hok, and Grandmaster Long.

The odd-looking group reached us, and Ling stuck out his hand to Phoenix. "Oh my goodness, young man. I had no idea you could ride like that. Mr. Chang and I are just . . . speechless."

"Thanks," Phoenix said. "I could never have done it without my friends, though. I mean it."

"We know," Ling said, shaking each of our hands.

"Congratulations to all of you! After a performance like that, how could we *not* offer all of you the opportunity to promote cycling throughout China? What do you say?"

Phoenix looked at his grandfather, and his grandfather smiled. "Yes!" Phoenix said. "A million times, yes!"

"Me too!" Hú Dié said. "It would be a dream come true."

Ryan looked as his mom, and she said, "Up to you, kiddo. I'll follow and support you wherever life takes you."

Ryan grinned. "Count me in, too, Coach! I'm looking forward to it!"

Everyone turned to me, and I frowned. I honestly didn't know what I wanted to do.

Ling cleared his throat. "Jake, I know we discussed you only coming here for one week, and I realize that most of your time here has been less than enjoyable, to say the least. However, we would be honored to have you stay here as long as you'd like and help us promote our cause. We've yet to select a location for our new state-of-the-art training facility, and a big part of the reason it's taking so long is that we've decided to include a world-class BMX track and a rec-reational BMX trail in the master plan. As you know, find-ing the right location with the right kind of dirt is crucial."

A lightbulb went off in my head, and I looked at Grand-master Long. It appeared as though the same lightbulb had gone off in his head, too. He smiled broadly and nodded at me.

I looked back at Ling. "How would you and Mr. Chang feel about building your new facility off the beaten path?"

"How far off the beaten path?"

"Outside of Kaifeng, in the mountains. The closest town is a cool little place known as—"

"Tea Village!" Ling said. "I know exactly the area you're talking about! Mr. Chang is a tea connoisseur, as am I. We travel there together several times each year. The air is clean and the surroundings are beautiful! It would be perfect!" He spoke excitedly to Mr. Chang in Chinese, and Mr. Chang's face broke into a wide smile. Everybody seemed pleased with the idea.

"As you can see," Ling said, "Mr. Chang loves the concept. There aren't many roads out there, but we have some money set aside for civil infrastructure. After all, we plan to make this a world-renowned destination."

"World-renowned?" Grandmaster Long asked.

Ling turned to him and eyed the old man's orange robe.

"Of course!" Ling said suddenly. "The fabled Cangzhen Temple, where the famous Five Ancestors once lived! Is it *real*?"

"Very real," Grandmaster Long replied. "And it can be yours, as long as you agree to teach kung fu as part of your training curriculum."

"That's a brilliant idea!" Ling said. "It will promote core strength, which is critical for elite cyclists. How much land are we talking about, and what might the cost be?"

"Hundreds of acres, and if you agree to restore our crumbling buildings to their former glory along with incorporating kung fu into the regimen, you can have it all for free."

Ling stuck out his hand. "You have yourself a deal, Mr. . . . ?"

"Long. Grandmaster Long."

They shook hands, and Ling turned to me.

"Thank you for this, Jake. As you can imagine, I'm more excited than ever to have you join our team. I can even arrange it so that you're the one who designs all of our BMX facilities. What do you say?"

I shook my head. "I'm not qualified to design anything, but I know someone who is."

"Raffi!" Phoenix, Ryan, and Hú Dié shouted in unison.

"Yes, Raffi!" Ling said. "The boy with the amazing dreadlocks. I remember him from California. We can bring him here, certainly. Is there anything else you would like?"

I thought about it for a second. "A dumpling stand. One that serves *xiao long bao.*"

Ling laughed. "I *told* you I've never met anyone who doesn't like our dumplings! We can certainly arrange that. So, will you join us and race BMX?"

"I don't know about racing," I said, "but sure, I'll join the team for at least a year and coach other riders and stuff like that."

"Yes!" Ryan said.

"Whoo-hoo!" Hú Dié cried. "I know what I am going to do to express my thanks to you! Build you a custom BMX bike!"

Phoenix smiled at me. "Nice. I guess you get the honor of being the one to make Cangzhen Temple rise out of the ashes."

"Oh, I don't know about that," I said with a grin. "I just want to ride my bike, bro!"

About the Author

Jeff Stone grew up in Michigan, but he has spent the past dozen years in Indiana with his wife and two children. He holds a black belt in Shaolin-Do kung fu, which he tested for at the legendary Shaolin Temple in China. He's ridden mountain and road bikes for years, but he bought his first BMX bike at age forty-three. His tail taps are pretty sick, but everything else is sketchy.